DARK EMPORIUM – VOLUME 2

Edited by Misty Coleman

DARK EMPORIUM – VOLUME 2

FICTION4ALL

ISBN: 978 1 78695 882 2

Published by
Fiction4All
www.fiction4all.com

This Edition
Published 2024

TABLE OF CONTENTS

The Backroad Butcher (Rie Sheridan Rose)

Billy Roy Jenkins drove with his knees down the dark, tree-lined, two-lane road. He perfumed the air with the cigarette held out of the driver's window, chugging hooch from the flask in his right hand. Life was good.

A flash of movement in his headlights startled him into full alertness. The cigarette dropped to the black tar road, and he spared a second to hope it would go out without causing any trouble. The flask fell to the passenger floorboard, the acrid aroma of moonshine wafting up as its remaining contents trickled out.

Billy Roy peered into the darkness, trying to see past the dim beams of the ancient headlights. There—off to the side of the road. Someone stood there.

He screeched the truck to a stop. Leaning out the window, he called, "Hey there. You okay? It's awful late and dark to be out here alone."

The figure turned toward him, and he blinked. "That you, Suzie June? What are you doing out here?"

The girl in the black dress moved closer to the truck, her skin bone-white in the headlights. Her hair hung in lank black strands, framing a face dominated by wide, dark eyes. "Billy Roy?" she breathed. "What are you doing here?"

7

"Just driving. Pretty girl like you shouldn't be out after dark alone. Haven't you heard about the Backroad Butcher?"

"I've heard. No choice, though. Still need to get home."

"Well, hop in. I'll take you home. I go right by there."

"Thank you. It is getting late." Suzie June walked around the front of the truck. Kind of glided. It struck Billy Roy as rather…Otherworldly.

Reaching across the cab, he opened the passenger door, and Suzie June slipped into the truck.

"Y'all still over on County Road 10?" he asked, acutely aware of her nearness as she settled into place. "Sorry, the truck's such a mess." He threw a couple of burger wrappers out the back window into the bed.

"Don't worry about it." She favored him with the ghost of a smile. "It's awful nice of you to stop for me."

"Happy to help."

They drove in silence for a few minutes while Billy Roy tried to work out a decent conversation starter.

"So…you goin' to the dance on Saturday?" he blurted out, when the silence got too thick to handle.

"I don't dance anymore."

"But you're such a great dancer!"

"Not anymore."

Silence descended once again. Wracking his brain for something else to talk about, Billy Roy returned to the only other topic that came to mind.

"How many kills has the Butcher tallied now? Four, five?"

"Six," she murmured.

"Jeez. How crazy do you gotta be?"

She turned to stare out the window at the trees flowing by. "You don't know what can drive a person."

Billy Roy gave up trying to make conversation, sullenly focusing on the road.

"Next left," Suzie June said.

He screeched the truck around the curve without comment. The road devolved into a dirt track with mud ruts jarring the undercarriage of the truck. They bounced along for several minutes before he pulled to a stop outside a ramshackle cabin with the requisite number of broken-down vehicles scattered about the bare earth yard. An aura of sadness seemed to permeate the area, and Billy Roy—not usually sensitive to such things—shivered.

"Wanna come in for a bit?" Suzie June asked, her voice hesitant. "We don't get many visitors way out here. I'm sure Pa will want to thank you for bringing me home."

Billy Roy weighed his options. Nothing but homework waited for him at home. Ma was working the late shift tonight and wouldn't even know he was gone. "Sure. Why not? You can tell me why you ain't dancing anymore."

Suzie June seemed about to answer, but she stepped onto the rickety porch instead and opened the door. "Pa," she called, her voice soft and low, "I brought you some company."

9

She turned to Billy Roy. "Come on in. I'll fix us something to drink."

Billy Roy hesitated. Something was off about this whole thing. He'd been to Suzie June's before, but he'd never been inside. Even from the porch, he caught the miasma of untended garbage and some other stench—deeper, rusty, disturbing—underneath that odor.

"Maybe I should take a raincheck, Suzie. Ma will wonder where I am. I promised to bring home dinner."

"You won't be long, Billy. I just want you to try Pa's new batch of moonshine. He's working up a new mix. Thought you'd be interested." She shrugged.

It proved just the right lure. Billy Roy could never resist a new batch of shine, and everyone for twenty miles around knew it. Misgivings thrust aside, he stepped past Suzie June into the cabin.

The interior was almost as dark as the outdoors. Only one bare bulb in a floor lamp burned across the expanse of the living room. It couldn't have been more than a 40-watt bulb. Just enough light to see where he put his feet. The only other light came from a television playing a game show at so low a volume he couldn't even make out which one.

He caught sight of a vague shape in the worn recliner beside the lamp. It didn't move, even when Billy called a hearty, "Ev'nin', Mr. Summers."

The eerie itch something here didn't seem right prickled between his shoulder blades again, and Billy Roy turned, only to find Suzie June standing

10

right behind him with two brimming mason jars of clear liquid.

"Here's your shine, Billy. Go sit there on the couch by Pa, and I'll rustle up a snack to go with it."

"You don't need to go to that trouble, Suzie," he began, trying to inch around her.

"I insist, Billy." Her eyes flashed in the dim light. She thrust one of the mason jars into his hand and moved past him to set the other on the arm of the recliner. "Here you go, Pa," she murmured.

Billy sat on the edge of the sofa, holding the jar between his knees. He took one sip when she glanced his way expectantly.

Damn. The shine tasted phenomenal. It had a hint of something he couldn't define beneath the usual sharp taste. There seemed to be a bit of fruitiness as well, which made it go down easier than the rotgut he'd been drinking earlier.

Suzie June was still watching him, so he took another sip. Why the hell not?

He chugged the entire jar. It tasted so damn good…

Mr. Summers still hadn't moved in his scruffy old recliner. How could he resist the aroma wafting up from his own jar of hooch?

"Well, I really should get moving, Suzie J. My ma will ground me for a month if I don't get my homework done before she gets home."

"I thought she expected you to bring home dinner."

"Uh, yeah. She does."

"But she's not home? Billy, I'm disappointed in you. At least get your lies straight."

Billy rose to his feet and stumbled into the recliner, knocking the jar of moonshine off the arm and into Mr. Summers' lap. The old man still didn't react.

"Whaz goin' on here, Suzie June?" Billy slurred, blinking his eyes, trying to focus.

"Nothing to worry about, Billy Roy," she murmured. "Why don't you lie back on the couch there for a few minutes?"

"I gotta go," he protested, but his legs wouldn't obey his commands. "Maybe for a few."

He collapsed onto the couch in a heap. His head spun like the merry-go-round in the playground at the church. What the hell was happening here?

Suzie June looked down at him, her head cocked to the side. "Yes, I think you will be a delightful addition to the family."

"What are you talkin' about?"

"Well, there's Pa there—" She pointed at the recliner. "Oh, I bet you need a bit more light to see him properly." She flicked a switch on the wall, and the room sprang into sharp focus with the addition of the floodlights in each corner.

Billy Roy gasped as he got his first clear look at the figure on the recliner. The man looked almost skeletal—or maybe mummified was a better description. A wound in his neck gaped like a second smile. His clothes appeared stiff with blood and other fluids.

"What happened, Suzie?"

12

"He didn't want me to go dancing, Billy…so he did this." She lifted her skirt to disclose the rough wooden feet attached to her legs. They looked odd…like rocking chair runners more than proper feet. Maybe that explained the weird gliding motion.

"Well, I couldn't put up with that, now, could I?" she continued. "He expected it would keep me home. So, I showed him how I felt about that. And I liked it. Made me feel powerful. Special. So, now I look for people who need to learn a lesson—and I teach it to them."

"What?" Billy found it more and more difficult to keep his eyes open. "What have you done?"

"Haven't you figured it out yet, Billy Roy?" She shook her head with a sigh. "I thought you were smarter than that. You shouldn't have been out joyridin' tonight, Billy. Then I would have found myself another loser to teach. But you come barreling down the road like you owned it. You don't. I do. Guess this will up my count to seven. Always been my lucky number."

She stepped forward, with that strange gliding step. The last thing Billy Roy saw was the glint of steel in her hand.

The Dispossessed (Paul Edwards)

I spent days plotting how I was going to infiltrate Kirstie Langford's life.

Most nights I would gaze up at her window, at the pale, dim light inside her room. Sometimes I'd catch sight of her – a shadow, a flicker; as fleeting and insubstantial as a ghost. Then she'd turn and slip out of my sight again.

Sometimes I'd almost feel something. A residue; a trace, perhaps. Memories of Sara would re-surface: her face, her smile, her voice.

"What are you thinking about?" Kirstie asked.

I looked up from my pint. The wood-panelled walls of the Cross Keys Inn snapped back into focus.

"Nothing," I replied.

I was quiet for a moment. I rubbed my eye with the palm of my hand. "It's just… Well, this is kind of weird for me. To be out with you…with anyone like this." I painted on a thin smile. "I've been watching you for quite a while now."

"I know," she said.

I stared out the window at the monochrome grey sky.

"This is the first time I've asked anyone out since my wife…left."

It was impossible to feel bad about the lie.

"Sorry," I said quickly, raking a hand through my hair, "I didn't mean to bring her up."

"It's okay," she said, taking a sip of her wine. "You can talk about her if you like. I don't mind."

"She was my everything," I continued, my voice emotionless. "I would have done anything for her. But I just didn't see... I..."

She narrowed her eyes. "You can't let go?"

I nodded.

"I think I understand," she said, looking down at her hands. "When did you break up?"

"About seven years ago. She went to Sydney, Australia, to live with another man. I tried to find her out there. Spent months just...searching."

"My husband left me a year ago," she said, quietly, and half-smiled.

She reached out a hand, smoothed my knuckles with her fingers.

We went back to her place.

In her room she sat on her bed as I gazed about me. It was pretty much how I had expected it to be. Old, peeling wallpaper; a small narrow bed pushed up against the wall; a pot of flowers on a desk; a round makeup vanity mirror. The room smelt of potpourri and a sweet, inexpensive perfume.

I looked at her, and she looked at me with those immensely lonely eyes. She pushed her hands between her thighs and said, "Come sit by me."

I stepped toward her. "There's something I have to tell you," I said. "I'm incapable of feeling. And I...miss her, you know? I know I miss her."

I stopped and plucked a photograph out of my jacket pocket. It was of Sara, smiling that pretty smile of hers.

"Is that her?" Kirstie asked. "Is that your wife?"

"Yes," I said.

"May I look?"

I shook my head.

There were other pictures in my pocket. Love letters, too. I took them out and laid them on the floor, right next to her feet.

"What are you doing?" There was a slight tremble in Kirstie's voice.

"I used to be like you," I said, straightening up, sitting down on the bed beside her at last. "I had a good life. I have memories. No feelings, though. Not anymore."

I cast wide, vacant eyes upon her. "I don't know how it happened, but I'm not human anymore. I can only siphon, see. And what you've got... Well, the pain makes it real, you know?"

My fingers brushed her blouse, her skin. She screwed her eyes up tight. Then my hand passed right through her, groping, reaching, searching the space beyond.

Kirstie's head lolled sideways, her eyelids flickering.

It didn't take me long to find what I was searching for.

I withdrew my hand, Kirstie tumbling right off the bed. I knelt beside her unmoving form and stared at all my pictures of Sara on the floor.

Suddenly, a wave of grief came crashing over me. My body shook, my stomach churned. I glanced across at the mirror, tears shattering my image in the glass. I scrunched photographs and love letters under me as I screamed and wept into the carpet.

Rolling on to my back, I moaned her name, over and over: Sara, Sara, Sara.

In time, it subsided.

I sat up, dazed and disorientated.

I stared at the photographs scattered around me.

I felt nothing again.

The police found Kirstie five days later, but by then I'd moved on. I was in another city, another place, looking for girls who were weighed down by the world. It's not too hard to pick out the lonely, the broken, the dispossessed.

One afternoon I was sat in a park when a pale girl passed me by. She was tall and thin, with blond hair that made me think of Sara. As she walked past, she glanced at me and smiled, although the smile never quite reached her eyes.

She hurried on.

I watched her for a moment, then got up and followed.

Now That I've Lost You (Paul Edwards)

I move to the window. Darkening headstones stand out against the bruised sky like cardboard cutouts.

You're wearing brown leather boots, a silk lilac dress, and dark, wrap-around sunglasses. Skeletons of trees whisper and sway around you.

You step up to the porch and I shrink back into the shadows of the room. A red lamp paints my face, like a hallucination, onto the darkness of the pane.

"I'm going to save you, Kate," I whisper, over and over, until it becomes a kind of mantra.

It started at a party Julian was throwing – a reunion for his old university mates.

Broomstick thin and ashen faced, dripping with runic pendants and bangles, he flitted from one person to another, bragging, smoking Camels and knocking back whisky.

"Where did you get those from?" asked a boy in a Bauhaus T-shirt.

Julian drew sharply on his cigarette, glancing up at the two ornate Samurai swords mounted on the wall. "Bought them in Osaka. Beautiful, aren't they?" A smile tugged at the corner of his mouth.

I fucking hated that smile.

In the kitchen, Kate's friend Scott was busy ransacking the fridge for beer. "Hi Mike," he said, straightening up. "Great party, eh?"

"Have you seen Kate?" I asked. "Can't seem to find her anywhere."

"No. 'Fraid not," he shrugged apologetically, the glare of the strip light accentuating his black, black eyes. "So, uh, how's things going between you and her?"

"Good. All good, mate."

"You're a lucky guy – Kate's an excellent girl. We used to share art classes Tuesdays and Thursdays. It was the three of us – me, Kate, and Julian."

I glanced into the hall. Couples were pressed against the stairs, their faces masked by darkness. "Julian's a popular guy," I said.

"He's one cool fucking dude. I mean, take a look at this house. I would kill to have a place like this."

He moved to the window, rubbing the fog away with the palm of his hand. "Look out there – see the graveyard? This house used to be an old Methodist church. I mean, how fucking cool is that?"

Kate told me that Julian wrote his poetry out there; after sunset he'd lie on a tomb and smoke weed under the stars, jotting his visions down in a Book of Shadows.

I grabbed a beer and went searching for Kate upstairs. Along the landing huddled figures lay slumped under crimson lanterns like characters in a van Gogh nightscape. I inspected each face – Kate wasn't there.

A couple brushed past me on their way to a bedroom. The girl was laughing, teeth glinting in the darkness. I followed them. The room was dark, bare. Rob Zombie howled from a beaten stereo. Crouched upon the carpet, silent and stoned, a bunch of teenagers passed around a bottle wrapped in brown paper.

I drifted to the window. Moonlight illuminated Kate, sitting beneath the wings of a crumbling stone angel. She was with Julian and they were laughing and he had his arms around her and they didn't even notice me.

Two days before Christmas, we went shopping in the city centre. As we came out of a department store the bus was waiting for us, shivering by the kerb. We squeezed into the seats at the back and Kate took hold of my hand.

Blurred shadows flitted past the windows. Clouds trembled, flaking snow. "What are you thinking about?" Kate asked.

I turned to her. "What's going on between you and Julian?"

Her mouth opened, but for a few seconds she couldn't speak. "What? What do you mean?"

"You've been spending a lot of time with him just lately."

She snatched her hand back. "What exactly are you getting at, Mike?"

"I saw you two together at the party. You were all over him."

She turned away, disgusted, but I couldn't see her reflection in the darkness of the pane.

Later, curled up in bed together, she relented. She shook me, to wake me, but I was awake anyway. "Mike," she said. "I haven't been entirely straight with you."

I sat up. She drew her coppery hair away from her eyes. "I did have a relationship with Julian, but that was way before you. We only lasted a few weeks. It's a miracle our friendship survived, really. So yes, we are close – and you'll just have to accept it. But as a couple, Julian and I are over, okay?"

I felt sick and scared. Betrayed. "Why didn't you tell me about this before?" I asked.

"I…I didn't want you to worry about it. I love you, Mike, and as crazy as this sounds, I worry about what you think of me. But I don't want to have to hide anything from you ever again." She puffed out her cheeks. "That's why it's important for me to tell you this."

She smiled.

In the darkness, her face seemed paler than usual. Smudges of purple sat raw around her black, black eyes.

Julian popped around one evening to give Kate some of his poetry to read. I watched him from the other end of the hall, standing in the shadows of the doorway, his emaciated frame enveloped in a black leather coat. They were whispering something, but I couldn't quite hear what they were saying over the sound of the rain on the rooftiles.

After he'd gone, Kate curled up in her armchair to read his poetry. Her face was scrunched up in concentration, her mind lost to his words.

21

Looking back, it wasn't the exchange of bodily fluids that bothered me; it was the interchange of thoughts and dreams that concerned me more. You see, these things can open a person up...

They can bind people together for eternity.

Twilight crept through gnarled trees.

I crouched in the gloaming, watching Kate and Julian drift through the graveyard, her head on his shoulder, their fingers entwined. As he talked, Kate's hair licked and whipped about her face, coppery threads writhing in the air like snakes.

Leaves rustled, trees creaked. Marble angels glared at me with their hollowed-out eyes.

He gripped her hands, shuffled in close, whispered into her ear. I couldn't breathe. Then his mouth found her neck, her eyelashes fluttering and her head lolling as his long black coat enveloped them both.

I blinked tears, stared up at the sky, at dark, blood-washed trees.

I woke suddenly that night.

Kate was asleep, her coppery hair fanned out across the pillow.

As I gazed at her, I noticed how unnaturally white her face looked in the moonlight.

Her eyes snapped open. She looked disorientated, confused. "Where are you?" she whispered, her hands reaching for my face.

The room went black. From behind the curtains a shadow passed across the face of the moon.

I froze. Then moonlight streamed through the curtains again, and I turned back to Kate. She was barely breathing.

I touched her throat, feeling for holes.

We spent last Sunday in our little rented house, trying to save us.

We sat on our sofa, the rain clawing angrily at the windowpane. I tried listening beyond the rain, but I couldn't hear her breathe. She was smoking Camels, one after the other.

I wanted to ask her if she was going to see him again, whether she was going to sneak over there after work. But what was the point?

Then it hit me. This wasn't Kate. This thing sat next to me wasn't the woman I'd loved.

"Why did you tear up my stuff?" she asked, her eyes fixed on nothing in particular on the wall.

In the bedroom, the window banged loudly in the wind. Shredded pieces of poetry swirled across the floorboards.

I didn't say a thing. Instead, I thought about the key I'd found in her handbag, and how I'd taken a copy of it at the local hardware store.

And so here I wait for you, Kate. So, so patiently I wait.

I never dreamed I'd hurt you. I never dreamed I'd lose you. Not in a thousand years. Not in an eternity.

But you were taken from me and violated. Now, you're less than real.

You're not even human.

Click.

You let yourself in.

You call his name – once, twice; then make your way upstairs. I hold my breath. Behind me, Julian's body lies broken on the bed. His head stares up at me from across the bedroom floor.

Floorboards creak on the landing.

"I'm going to save you, Kate."

I grip the Samurai sword in my hand.

The door opens.

Evelyn (Chris Rodriguez)

"Here ya go, Angel! A nice treat for being a good girl." Ted handed his Cockatoo her snack bar of seeds and honey. Angel was his girl. The only female he would consider living with at this time of his life.

Theodore enjoyed his apartment at Cottonwood Cove Retirement Community. For the most part. There were a lot of women here. Back in the day, he would have enjoyed living around a lot of women. More opportunities to strut his stuff. But after a couple of divorces that stripped him of his possessions and pride, he had been ready to give up on a life that included women. His saving grace was he had always enjoyed his own company more than a relationship with anyone else, including with most other men. His relationships with people never lasted long.

"Don't get me wrong, Angel," Ted said as he stroked her breast. "I like the people here. Some are very nice, but I just don't want to live with any of them. Especially that Evelyn!"

Angel laughed raucously. "EVelyn! EVelyn! Eat this Evelyn!"

"Sshhh!" Ted put a finger on her beak. "Not so loud." He stroked her affectionately. "You are one smart bird though."

A scratching and scrabbling out on his deck made Ted spin around so quickly he tripped over his own feet and almost fell. He windmilled his arms to gain balance as he grabbed a tennis ball from a bowl on his coffee table and ran for the sliding glass doors. But before he could launch the rubber missile at the squirrels crossing his balcony rail, they jumped to safety across to Evelyn's deck to feast on the assortment of peanuts and leftovers she threw out for what she called her "wild babies" consisting of various birds and squirrels.

"Damn that woman!" Ted glared at the mess the disgusting creatures had dropped on his deck, and not just shells, but piles of poop pellets. "Damn those fluffy-tailed rats!" Ted, better than anyone in this building, knew that squirrels were rodents. He had owned Theodore's Pest Control business for 40 years. He was eternally astonished that people would call him screaming about mice or rats in their house or on their property, but thought squirrels were cute and fed them like pets. He tried fruitlessly for all those years to educate people about the disease they carried and the damage they inflicted daily to property and gardens. He wasted money on campaign booklets explaining that these squirrels weren't even native to our region, lobbying the city council to do something to allow him to rid the community of this pestilence. All to no avail. It only rallied citizens to protest his business. And his second wife to divorce him. He almost went bankrupt. He only survived because they had to call him to rid their homes of Hobo Spiders (thank you, Lord, for driving them into our region), Box Elder Bugs and termites at the very least.

A few days later at Bridge Club, he and Evelyn had words.

26

"I've had to clean my deck off three times this week! I didn't invite those nasty critters up to my place. Why don't you stop feeding them on your deck. Take the food out to the lawn or under a tree or something."

Evelyn sniffed and casually stroked the solid white streak in the middle of her grey hair as she studied her cards. "I'm not going to argue with you today, Theodore. I'm in a good mood for a change."

"All I'm asking..." he started, but was interrupted by Wanda, the Activities Director.

"Ted. We've had this discussion before. We all voted that Evelyn could do whatever she wanted to support the wildlife community on her own balcony."

"That's my point!" Ted raised his voice, but immediately closed his mouth as he glanced around for any kind of support from the others. None. He shuffled his feet, stayed quiet for the rest of the hand, then got up and left. "Not fair," he mumbled as he turned his back on the group.

"We've got to make a plan, Angel," he told his perfect little lady. "Somehow, some way, we have got to get rid of that woman. Make her want to move. Get her away from my apartment."

"Eat this, Evelyn!" Angel replied. Agitated by her owner's mood, she swished her beak through the tray of seeds and fruit, scattering it onto the floor which fortunately was covered in an easy-to-clean plastic floor covering.

"Dang it, Angel!" Ted bent to sweep up the mess with the whisk broom hanging nearby. "Don't you start, too!"

Angel flapped her wings and stretched up tall on her perch, bobbing her head so her crest raised and flattened. "So sorry. So sorry."

"Yeah, right," Ted mumbled. Then he stood and smoothed the bird's neck feathers and kissed her on the beak.

Later in the week, Ted went down to shoot some pool with a few of the guys in the building. He was hoping to bring up his predicament, but old Chester Garcia shut him down before he could get a word out.

"You shouldn't be so hard on Evelyn," he said before he broke the balls. Three of them dropped so he paused to eye the table before setting up his next shot. "She's a really nice lady and everybody loves her. You're fighting a losing battle, buddy."

Ted sighed and sat back on a stool as Chet dropped his next three balls and it looked like it might be a while before it would be his turn. *Good thing we're not playing for bucks today.* Ted took advantage of the days Chester forgot to take his medication and his big hands would shake like he was playing the maracas in a Mariachi Band.

"Besides, Lupe told me to read you the riot act and threatened to not let me play with you anymore if you keep bothering her friend."

"You're afraid of your wife, Chet?" was Ted's comeback.

Chet stopped adjusting the aim of his pool cue through his fingers and stood straight up. He turned slowly to face Ted. "Aren't you?"

The other guys snickered. They remembered quite clearly the confrontation Ted and Lupe had at the summer barbeque about whether or not the border should be closed to all Hispanics since the majority were drug runners and criminals. She turned nearly black in the face and drove her petite four-foot frame forward so forcefully, all six feet of Ted nearly backed into the flaming grill. He was almost charred through the seat of his pants before Chet rescued him and pulled Lupe off like she was a Pit Bull on crack cocaine.

"Why you worry about Evelyn, anyway?" Chet asked. "She's practically the oldest person in this building. She'll be gone soon enough."

Three days later, Ted instantly recalled that earlier discussion when they found Evelyn's body cold in her apartment.

She had left her balcony door open and unluckily slipped on what looked like squirrel poop on her kitchen floor. Her head hit the edge of the counter and split like a ripe melon. The pool of blood was tracked all over the apartment by the animals she fed. Her kitchen ransacked and packages of peanuts, seed and other wild critter snacks spread all over and out through the now filthy glass door.

Ted felt relieved and guilty at the same time. He knew it was inappropriate for him to feel in the least bit good that Evelyn would no longer be his neighbor under these circumstances. And in a way felt he had cursed her somehow. He licked his lips and his agitation was noted by his "lady."

"Uh, oh! Bad news. Uh, oh!" Angel flapped and fussed.

Ted ignored her and walked out to the balcony. He looked around and wondered how long it would take before the animals would stop coming to visit their benefactor. He couldn't wait for that ordeal to be over.

It took a couple weeks for a hired crew could go in to clean Evelyn's apartment after the police investigation once her body had been removed. The animals still came across Ted's deck to check for food at Evelyn's. And worse, they started stopping on Ted's deck to look at him through the glass doors. He angrily threw the tennis balls at the doors to scare them off until one bounced back and knocked poor Angel off her perch. She screamed bloody murder and flew at him. She wasn't tethered since he had just cleaned her cage and perch. He allowed her to be loose for a short time every day to properly stretch her beautiful wings. Ted held and calmed her before returning her to safety. He gave her some of her favorite fresh mango and apologized. "So sorry, Angel. So sorry."

After a few days of visits by more and more nasty critters outside his doors, he began to hatch a plan. Nobody can tell him he couldn't do anything about those dang verminous creatures now. He threw on a jacket and headed out the door to do some shopping.

"Why, Ted! Are you feeding Evelyn's animals now?" Lupe had come to fetch Chet for his scheduled physical therapy. "That's quite a change of heart," she commented. She looked at him slyly as if she didn't believe he could perform kind acts.

30

"So? What's it to you?" Ted threw back at her.

"That right, Ted?" Chet asked. "You feeding those squirrels you hate so much?"

Ted shuffled his feet nervously. He didn't know he had attracted so much attention to his project. That's not good.

"Come on, Lupe," Chet grabbed his wife's arm. "Let's leave ole Ted to his new hobby."

When Ted returned to his apartment, he opened the drapes on his sliding doors and saw a large squirrel sitting on the rail. Out of pure reflex, he hit the glass with his fist. The squirrel didn't flinch. She sat defiantly staring him down. The disturbing thing about this squirrel was she had a white stripe through the fur on her head. She flicked her tail, then hopped down to the bowl now sitting on the deck. It had been filled with nuts and seeds. She cautiously approached the bowl, took a sniff and turned to jump back onto the rail. Another squirrel dropped down from the branch that overhung Ted's balcony onto the railing. It sat and watched Ted for a minute, then jumped down to walk to the bowl. The big squirrel hissed at it making it jumped back.

Ted was intrigued and decided he was going to hate this new squirrel even more than the others. The white stripe on its head reminded him of something and it suddenly dawned on him.

"Evelyn!" he said out loud. Did his neighbor's ghost possess a squirrel? He shook his head. That's ridiculous. Still… "You have Evelyn's hair. I'm going to call you Evelyn you little demon."

The squirrels jumped back up into the branch and disappeared. A few birds landed near the bowl and pecked at the seed. Ted closed the drapes and went about his daily routine.

A couple of days later, Ted snuck out early in the morning to pick up dead birds from under his deck and scattered around the grounds. He was disappointed that no squirrel carcasses were found amongst the carnage. He refilled the bowl with only peanuts in shells this time and waited patiently. It wasn't long before squirrels were coming down out of the tree to gather on his deck. However, if any moved toward the bowl, the big squirrel, Evelyn, warned them away.

"EAT IT, Evelyn, you stupid squirrel!" Ted yelled in frustration. "How the hell does she know, Angel? How does Evelyn know?"

"Eat this, Evelyn!" Angel replied.

"Right, Angel." Ted smoothed her comb. "Good bird. You tell them."

The next day, there were even more squirrels, maybe a dozen sitting on the rail of Ted's balcony. They all stared silently into his apartment, not making a move toward the bowl still full of peanuts. Ted was growing impatient. He paced back and forth in his front room willing the squirrels to come down and eat from the bowl. Nothing. No action. He went to the sliding door and leaned against the glass staring back. The squirrels didn't move. More came down out of the trees and when the rail was full, they started sitting on the deck floor. They continued to make no movement except for occasionally flicking a tail or scratching an ear.

Ted couldn't stand it anymore. Evelyn and her gang of filthy rodents were taunting him. Goading him into taking some kind of action. Well, he was happy to oblige!

He grabbed a baseball bat from his closet and quietly slid the glass door open, picturing hitting a home run with each and every ball of fluff on his rails. He carefully closed the door behind him and expected the squirrels to scamper away from his presence. Instead, they sat quietly, staring him in the eye like little gunslingers ready to draw.

Ted chuckled at that. All these stupid, defenseless rodents armed and dangerous. "HA!" he laughed out loud. The sudden noise should have sent them scurrying, but it did galvanize them into action. Just not the kind Ted thought it would.

Evelyn let out a piercing squirrel scream and leapt off the rail at Ted's throat. She bit deeply into his neck, her surprisingly heavy body throwing him off balance. The rest of the pack jumped onto him then, each of them finding purchase with sharp claws and teeth. Ted's arms swung wildly, trying to find purchase to gain his balance. Nothing but air. He could hear Angel inside screaming, "Eat this, Evelyn!" as his body fell back against the rail. Ted reached to grab Evelyn and rip her off his throat. He felt her bones break in his hands, but too late. Blood spurted like a fountain from his throat as more squirrels climbed higher on his body, relentlessly gnawing at him until he went limp. The rail gave way under his weight. The squirrels leaped off as he fell. Ted felt like he was floating, moving in slow motion. It seemed to take forever to hit the sidewalk three stories down. He had time to try to scream, "Damn you, Evelyn!" but all that came out was a gurgle.

Three months later, the Strongman's moved into Ted's apartment. They were instantly popular as John Strongman was Evelyn's little brother and his wife was a whiz at Bridge. Once they were settled, Edna opened the sliding glass doors to place the deck chairs out in the sun. "Oh, look, John! There are squirrels! We need to pick up some bird seed and peanuts next time we shop.

Running (Rie Sheridan Rose)

My best friend Jake and I saw ourselves as Tom Sawyer and Huck Finn. From the time we could walk, we played together—cowboys and Indians, or pirates, or explorers…—you know, all the stuff boys do when they are young and stupid.

We were twelve that summer. The weather felt hot as hell. We stayed outside as much as possible, wearing as little as we could get away with, and haunting the swimming hole most of the day.

The weekend of the Fourth of July, we talked about plans for the fireworks that night as we swam.

"I bet they will have some of those big pinwheels. The kind that light up the sky like a flower and then rain down sparks," Jake said.

"Maybe. Grandpa bought me a pack of sparklers too, and Mom said we can light them after supper."

"Are we coming to your house for barbeque, or is everyone going to the park?"

"I can't remember. Let's go home and find out."

We swam to the edge of the pond and climbed out. The day felt blistering, so we cut through the trees down by the creek that fed the swimming hole. They arched above the water like a living tunnel. The shade helped cut the temperature a little.

When we rounded a bend in the creek, there stood two men yelling at each other. We ducked behind a bush because we didn't want to interrupt

35

what looked like a heated argument. One guy loomed tall and tan, with dark hair and a T-shirt reading "Nuke the Rich." The other appeared much shorter, with thinning blond hair and jeans torn out at the knees. He looked familiar, though I'd never seen the big one before.

The little one punched the tall one in the stomach, and then the tall one pulled a knife out of his pocket and stabbed the little one. The blond guy gasped and collapsed onto his knees, blood pouring out of his mouth in a red flood.

"Holy shit!" Jake cried, then clapped his hands over his mouth in horror.

The tall man glanced our way. His face crumpled into a scowl, and he snarled, "You kids! What the hell are you doing here?"

"Run!" I told Jake, and we took to our heels, running as fast as we could go.

I could hear the tall man crashing through the brush behind us, getting closer and closer. I made myself speed up.

Where could we go? Who was this guy? And who was the guy he'd killed—or at least hurt real bad?

I could hear Jake puffing along behind me. He was always a little slower and fatter than I was. He opened his mouth to speak—and I slashed a hand behind me. Talking wasn't an option right now.

My mind raced. We were twelve! What the hell could we do?

"You got any money?" I panted.

"Not...much..." he gasped.

36

I jerked my head toward an animal trail branching off the pathway. We darted down it. A cliff ran beside the trail, and we slid down it as quickly as possible. A cave at the bottom had provided a refuge for generations of kids. The opening proved tight even for twelve-year-olds. I slithered through it and jerked Jake inside when he stuck for a heart-stopping second.

A boulder stood beside the entrance, and we pushed it in front of the hole with grunts and strained muscles. It would buy us a little time.

We had played pirates and smugglers in the cave since we were six. It provided a welcome haven. No one knew this cavern better than we two. The passages got even smaller as they went back into the hillside, and we scurried through them as fast as we could fly.

The winding tunnel opened into a larger room again some ways back, and we squeezed through the opening like grapes in a press.

"We can rest here for a minute," I panted. "Is there any jerky stashed in the chest?"

We had a box where we stored "provisions" in the cave. It usually held comics and candy, but we had camped here overnight a few times this summer, so I knew it should be better stocked than usual at the moment.

"There's a bit," Jake answered, checking the box. "Two candy bars, a bottle of water, and half a box of granola bars, too." He pulled everything out and stuffed it into the backpack we had brought it in earlier in the month.

"How about the treasure?"

He checked the jar we stuck spare change and birthday money in. "Maybe thirty bucks."

We had been saving for two years.

I sighed. "It'll have to do. Put it in the bag."

"What are we going to do, Mike? Really? We just saw some guy kill another guy. He won't let us get away with that."

"We've got to get out of town. Maybe to Grandpa's house. He'll keep us safe and know what to do next. He's a judge, after all."

"But he's at your house for the Fourth."

"I know where his spare key is. We can call home when we get there."

Noises of rock battering rock echoed down the passageway.

"He's coming! C'mon!" I shoved him toward the back exit—the smallest hole yet.

I feared for a moment Jake wouldn't make it through, but he did—not without losing a lot of skin. Like I said, we had dressed for heat and swimming, not for cave exploration. I threw the backpack after him and dove through the hole.

The tunnel on the other side was short, and we came out into the sunlight again, blinking at the sudden brightness. We were much closer to town now but headed away from the safety of home and family. The bus station was just a street away. The money we had saved should be enough to get to Grandpa's in the next town over.

We gave the man behind the counter the quarters and dimes we had collected in the jar, and received two tickets, just in time to catch the bus waiting at the terminal. We climbed aboard and took the rear seat of the bus. The other passengers shot us some strange looks, but we ignored them, exchanging a high five instead.

As the bus pulled out of the station, we saw the tall man—filthy and bloodied—run up to the ticket counter. He stared after the bus, and we ducked down low, peeking over the back of the seat as he grew smaller and smaller with distance.

"Did he see us?"

"I don't think so, Jake. We'll be okay. Grandpa will sort everything out for us. I'm sure we'll be okay."

As the bus lumbered toward Grandpa's house, I hoped I wasn't lying. I'd never been a fugitive before...but it sure felt more exciting than playing pirates.

My Bottled Up Rage (John Kujawski)

People wouldn't feel so bad about my neighbors if I hadn't found the bottle. It was the powder that had an effect on me. If all hell broke loose, I'd say it all came back when I originally found it.

A great discovery wasn't actually on my mind when the magic started. I wasn't looking for much of anything, all I wanted to do was lay in bed. I had one of those headaches that made me wonder what would happen if someone cut my brain open. I wondered what the doctors might find; the source of my migraines?. I'd seen an article, often on my mind, which said migraines could come from bottled up rage. Whoever wrote that made it seem as if someone who kept all their anger inside should know it wasn't healthy and things like a pain in the side of the head could certainly wreck a day. On this day, though, I was taking the trash out at work - that's when I found the bottle.

I could tell it was a bottle right away and I probably wouldn't have thought much of it. The thing wasn't sitting by the dumpster. It was in the bushes. There was no label, it was just clear glass with a large amount of blue powder inside. My guess was drugs but it seemed unlikely. Perhaps it was a kids' toy but that would have made for an odd kids' game. It seemed so strange looking that I decided to grab it before I headed home and I ended up bringing the bottle with me for the drive.

That whole time I was in the car I kept thinking about the things in life that drove me crazy. I couldn't stand the neighbors next door. I couldn't stand their parties, the sound of drunks having a good time with a bunch of laughs. I hated finding the empty liquor bottles outside the next day. The whole thing made me sick to my stomach. It was bad enough having headaches but listening to the noisy people was a nightmare.

Anyway, I brought the bottle inside when I arrived home. It looked like something I'd dreamt up. It was if the powder was out of a fantasy film or part of a magic trick at the local carnival. I couldn't stop looking at it. Finally, I did something I maybe shouldn't have done. I decided to pull the cork out and ended up sprinkling some of the blue stuff on the floor. It reminded me of the time I dumped cinnamon all over the place so I could keep mice away. I knew they hated the smell. I thought of my neighbors as rats but I didn't think much would happen to a rat or a person if I dumped some of that powder. As soon as it hit the floor, I started to feel better.

I think my headache cleared up in an instant. Not only that, I was in a good mood. I was more relaxed and felt rested. I sprinkled a bit more of it in the hall and on the kitchen floor. I didn't use it all up but I did make a mess.

I have to say when I woke up the next day, my mind felt like it had been cleansed. I was still hungry and skinny and somewhat tired as usual but it wasn't long before I was very much alive and more energetic than I had been in the past year or two.

Driving to work was actually a good time that day and for once I didn't want to run anyone off the road. I breezed through work like it was nothing. I didn't have any pain in my head or anywhere else. I went to the local cafe on my lunch break and put away two sandwiches like they were nothing. I had an appetite like never before. Part of me wondered what would happen if I actually ate some of that powder from the bottle.

Still, as much as I liked that meal at the café, I thought about the bottles of alcohol they had for sale. It wasn't so much the fact they had drinks there but I missed watching the woman who made them. She was a stunning redhead and I loved watching her work. There was always something special about the way she moved. She could handle the liquor bottles and the glasses as if there was an art to it. I thought she was beautiful and so many occasions I had felt better when I was sick just from looking at her.

For some reason, the manager fired her one day. That was the end of that. He was some horrible looking chubby guy with a beard. I never liked it when he was around. I suppose he was a bit like my neighbors, he was a burden present during my work weeks when I had lunch breaks. Still, I had enjoyed my food that day.

When work ended that night and I headed back to my place, I knew the neighbors had been drinking booze out of wine bottles again. I could hear the partying but for some reason it didn't enrage me. The only thing I noticed when I opened my front door was that all the powder seemed to be gone. I wasn't sure if it had dissolved or what the reason for that was but I didn't find any of it around the places where I knew I'd sprinkled it.

I went over to the table where I'd been keeping the bottle. There seemed to be some left for me to use again. I'd made up my mind I wanted to use it and so I started dumping it all over the place. The neighbors were louder than ever but I was feeling happy. That powder even seemed to be a bit like striking a match. It triggered something in me right away. If it was a fire in my system then I figured it was a good type of fire. I didn't care what it was because I just wanted to feel better the way people feel when they consumed alcohol. This seemed to be better than alcohol and better than drugs.

The next day and the day after that were great. It was a repeat of a perfect twenty-four hours. Then it was a perfect forty-eight hours. The only thing I hated was the powder didn't seem to last. It always disappeared. It vanished just the way the pretty bartender had vanished when the manager made her disappear from my sight. There wouldn't be much left. I was running out fast and tried looking around the bushes at work to see if I could find another one but of course I couldn't. I began to feel frustrated.

I'd say it was sometime later in the week when the powder finally ran out altogether. Perhaps it was my patience that ran out with it and I had visions of enemies and neighbors and managers all swirling around in my brain. I'm not exactly sure what happened because I was not seeing blue powder but I had a feeling of fire and anger and pain inside me that I had never experienced. At some point it was almost as if I was in a trance and then I knew I had really fallen apart.

It was almost as if I had sensory overload of some kind. All sorts of different sounds went through my head and the lights in the room seemed to be flashing in a way that nearly blinded me. There was even a bitter taste in my mouth and then at one point it was almost as if some other type of sense had taken over and I could see the visions of everyone I knew that liked and didn't like and all the things that frustrated me. They appeared as images in the room. I suppose I even passed out for a moment but when I woke up I took action on my emotions right away. The damage I did was overwhelming.

There was no way the neighbors would be having a party anytime soon. I'd smashed out several of their windows. No doubt the flames coming out of their home were there because I lit the matches that caused them.

I still had that bottle, though. It was empty but it was going to be quite a weapon. I knew if I hit someone with it I could do some real damage.

If only more powder had turned up. That was the one thing I kept telling myself over again that I'd hope would happen. I just hated that the bottle was empty. I knew just what to do with empty bottles, though. I could find the manager at that cafe. There was no telling what using empty bottles as weapons against him would do. I was positive that I had to find out. It was the only thing that would make me feel better.

Faces in the Glass (Susan E. Rogers)

The bottom half of the antique oval mirror in the hallway was fogged over. Anne glanced at it on her way to the kitchen and was surprised to see the patch of gauzy condensation. The storm knocked the power out overnight but it had been back on since five and the house was warm enough. She wiped the fog away with the sleeve of her heavy fisherman's sweater. Her reflection squinted back at her as she tucked a loose strand of shaggy blonde hair behind her ear and wrinkled up her nose. Why had she thought such a short cut would look good on her? She peered at her unblemished face and smiled. Her complexion looked as fresh as when she turned twenty-one, nine years ago.

The window over the kitchen sink was clear and dry as she looked out on the aftermath of the snowstorm. The overcast sky draped a gray curtain over the snow. Drifts reached the bottom of the windows on the shed, sculpted in scalloped tiers by the wind, an undisturbed shroud over the dormant rose bushes beneath. The plows hadn't been out yet, not here eight miles from town. She didn't mind being so far, really. This was home, the only house she had ever lived in. When her parents retired, they took off to explore the country in a camping trailer, leaving her in charge. She enjoyed the freedom and the sense of responsibility.

She sighed. Usually, she welcomed the snow, but not today. Her friend Caroline had planned a birthday celebration for her this afternoon – lunch at that new Italian restaurant and then the Johnny Depp movie at the mall cinema. Now it would have to be postponed. She turned on the oven and rummaged in the pantry for a box of cake mix. If she couldn't go to the party, she'd make her own. After all, not every day was the big three-oh. She was spooning batter into the cupcake papers when she heard a knock, quick and urgent tapping on glass. A quick glance at the kitchen window revealed nothing. She reached into the oven with the cupcake pan.

"Damn!" The burnt tip of her index finger jumped straight to her mouth as the door banged shut and her foot kicked out at the front of the stove. Her distorted image in the chrome of the faucet caught her eye as her finger cooled under cold running water. She waved it in the air and set the timer.

There was that knock again. Anne pulled the curtain back an inch from the narrow window alongside the front door but there was nothing to see. The snow was pristine. She shook her head and dropped the curtain back into place. Maybe a bird flapped up against the glass, or a loose wire was caught in a breeze. She shrugged and turned toward the living room to watch the local news and get an update on the forecast.

Condensation covered the whole mirror now. Her reflection was veiled and the gold frame was crooked. She reached out to straighten it and the knock sounded again, only louder. She jumped back. Something had rapped against the glass. Clear spots showed where knuckles had dabbed away the condensation. Suddenly, an invisible finger traced her name backwards in the fog from the inside – A-N-N-E.

She backed up until her butt hit the opposite wall, her eyes fixed to the image. Her own face peered back through the fog. A fingernail tapped on the glass from the inside. She slid down the wall as her reflected eyes followed her descent through the mirror's glass.

Anne had no idea how long she stayed there crouched against the wall. When the trance finally dissipated, she looked up at the mirror. The face—her face—was gone. The condensation was cleared. All she could see was the reflection of the framed sunset hung on the yellow wall above her head. Her feet were pins and needles. She used the wall for support and managed to stand, but it took several minutes of shaking her legs before she could take a step. The smell of burnt cupcakes wafted from the kitchen. She scooted sideways, never taking her eyes from the empty mirror, until she reached the doorway.

The cupcakes were black and beyond edible. She dumped them in the trash and flung the pan in the sink. What she needed was a cup of tea to settle her down. The endless monotone of snow through the window mesmerized her as she waited for the water to boil.

A piercing shrill from the kettle startled her awake. Her head flicked to clear the haze from her vison but caught in mid-shake. Her own face looked back at her through the window, frozen on the blank canvas of snow. The lips flared and the eyes bulged. Anne blinked and ran to the hallway. Her own face screamed at her from inside the mirror, the voice blotted out by the wail of the kettle. Two hands splayed against the inside of the glass.

Her hand inched toward the image and she frowned with fingers stopped just short of touching the mirror. She wasn't ready yet. It wasn't supposed to be here, but there might not be another opportunity and it would be foolish to ignore this one. Anne drew in her breath and held it as she placed her open palms against those of her reflection.

An instant surge of energy, blinding as a lightning strike, obliterated Anne's sight. An unseen force sucked at her hands and threatened to pull her into the glass. With feet planted against the wall, she leaned backwards and rocked on her heels. The force held fast. She pulled back and released, pulled back and released. Finally, a slight lessening. Her leg and back muscles tensed. She hunched forward, then heaved backwards with all her might.

A deafening crack preceded a thunderous pop. The suction hold released and Anne tumbled backwards against the opposite wall. A heavy weight held her down. Flashes of fireworks exploded before her eyes. A shrieking whistle pierced her ears. She could only lie there, defenseless against whatever had broken through the mirror into her world.

A few minutes passed before Anne's vision cleared. Her eyes raised reflexively to the mirror. The glass was clouded over with milky white. A woman lay across her legs, heavy and motionless. Tentatively at first, Anne raised her knees as much as she could, an inch or two at most, and started to bounce them under the limp body ever so slightly, alternating from one leg to the other. She tapped the shoulder closest to her. A faint shudder ran through the person from head to feet. Anne grinned and tapped with a bit more pressure, then again, harder.

The woman trembled and her two hands slid to the floor. The body jerked up on stiffened elbows. The woman lifted her head and a ribbon of slimy drool dripped from the corner of her mouth onto Anne's sweatpants. Their eyes met. The exact same eyes, blue with tiny gold flecks.

"Thank you." The woman's voice fluttered like the whispered rasp of sandpaper against chalk as she pushed herself to her knees, slipped forward but tried again and settled backwards on her heels. "You're my..."

"Reflection. Yes." Anne pushed herself up and extended a hand. "Come on. I'll get you something to soothe your throat before you try to talk anymore."

The woman grabbed onto Anne and managed to stand. Anne turned and tugged, until she followed along into the kitchen. The kettle was still whistling and Anne shut it off. She reached into the cupboard for two mugs and the box of lavender tea.

Soothing aroma curled around them. The woman cleared her throat after three sips of the hot brew. Anne took a slow drink from her cup and waited. The two stared at each other for several seconds. They wore the same off-white sweater and

50

gray sweatpants, their hair was cut in the same short shag and their hands held the mugs in the same pose. The woman looked around the kitchen and her gaze landed on the gray snowscape beyond the window. Anne smirked and put her mug down on the table.

"So, what was that all about?"

The woman lowered her eyes and stared at her tea. "I'm not sure." Her voice was still low, but the scratchiness was gone.

"You know you came here through the mirror, right?"

"I guess so, but I don't know how. Did you make me come through?"

"Uh-huh. I did." Anne nodded.

"I was scared. There was something really dangerous—really… evil. I felt it trying to get me. I couldn't see anything, only you… or, uh, me… through the mirror." The woman took a sip and swallowed slowly. "Is your name Enna too?"

"No, it's Anne." She laughed. "But you're not the only one."

Enna frowned and blinked. She shook her head and looked around the room. "It looks just like my kitchen." Her eyes settled on Anne. "So, am I in some kind of alternate universe? It all feels familiar and strange at the same time." She picked up the mug and tapped it on the table. "And real, even though it's all a reflection."

"I guess you could call it that. But to me, you're the reflection, not the other way around."

51

"Oh." Enna cocked her head and scrunched her forehead as she thought about that. "But I'm real, so how can you be, too?"

Anne snorted and shrugged. "So, what was the evil? Did you see something?"

"No. I just felt this… this… presence." Enna's eyes widened and she shivered. "It felt so dark and threatening. It got really, really cold and… and… I thought somebody was behind me, like eyes watching every move I made."

"Why didn't you leave the house?"

"I couldn't." Enna's eyes darted toward the window. "Because of the snow. I was trapped in the house. Like you. At least I'm safe here."

Anne nodded. A smirk crossed her lips but she coughed and hid her mouth with her fist.

"It's my birthday today," Enna said. "It must be yours, too. Thirty, right?"

"It certainly is," said Anne as she rose from the table. "Just stay here and drink your tea. I've got to take care of something. I'll be right back."

"Sure," said Enna. "Maybe we can celebrate our birthday together later."

"Oh, we certainly will." Anne grinned and headed to the hall.

Enna waited a few seconds then peeked out through the kitchen doorway. The other woman was out of sight. She started to open cabinets and drawers, but didn't find anything like she was looking for as she rummaged through dishes and cooking equipment. A door on the other side opened into a pantry cupboard, filled with cans and boxes of food. She hadn't really believed what she needed would be in the kitchen, but she had to check while she had the chance. She'd have to figure out some ploy that would give her an opportunity to search the other rooms in the house. She was certain that Anne had fallen for her act so far. She grinned and nodded as she sat at the table and took another sip of tea.

Anne glanced at the old mirror on the way down the hall. It was still clouded over. Enna would probably be her only shot at the birthday ritual today, even though everything had happened out of order. Enna wasn't supposed to appear so soon. Anne hadn't even performed the spell to summon her yet. She knew much of the ritual was her own invention and not really necessary. But she liked it—liked the tradition of it. Every year since her thirteenth birthday, she had called forth an Enna in the old mirror. This year was different, the reflection came first. And, for the first time, the reflection was a living person, talking and walking in her kitchen. Anne was surprised that this Enna seemed rather naïve and wimpy, almost insulted that her reflection should lack her own strength of character.

The door to the spare room squeaked open on seldom-used hinges once Anne unlocked it with her special key. Soft light glowed from the overhead chandelier when she flicked the switch. Faceted glass teardrops hung from the ornate light and speckled the walls with kaleidoscopes of color that swayed in the slight breeze when the door swung open. It was a small room, no bigger than a walk-in closet, but it held her secret and she had the only key.

Anne glanced at the floor to ceiling mirror that covered the entire wall on her left. The image of everything in the room was echoed there, except her own reflection. The mirrored wall served a different purpose—to keep watch over the ones confined here. She slipped another key into a switch and the full-length black velvet curtain that covered the opposite wall rose in one smooth motion toward the ceiling. Behind the drapery, seventeen identical cedar-framed mirrors hung on the wall, the gallery of her conquests over the years. Soon, the eighteenth would join them. She pivoted to face them and scanned each one in turn.

Seventeen faces—her face in each mirror—stared back at her. She grinned as her gaze drifted to the one on the far left. That was her first, from the day she turned thirteen—the year she reached puberty and the power to command her reflection manifested in her. At first it was simply fun, but she soon realized that each captured Enna relinquished its youth to her. As each birthday passed with her reflections trapped in the mirrors, it became clear that her aging had slowed far more than it should have with the chronological passing of time. She wasn't getting younger, but she hadn't grown any older.

Her thirteen-year-old face stared back at her, stalled forever in teeny-bopper innocence, blond hair long and straight with bangs fallen into wide eyes of disbelief. She was the very first Enna that Anne had sucked from another plane and imprisoned in the glass here. Tears welled in this young Enna's eyes. One overflowed and spilled

54

down a pale cheek as Anne watched. The teen began to sob silently, her mouth stretched downward and her shoulders quaking. Anne giggled.

Her eyes slid from that image to the next and then the next, each in turn, subtle changes in appearance and style from year to year. Emotion varied from face to face, blazing through the glass, each expression a vivid portrait. Age fifteen Enna who watched Anne's every movement, eyes squinted and nose wrinkled with disgust. Twenty-year-old Enna with tears sluicing down her cheeks as she mouthed a voiceless "please, please" over and over. Enna at twenty-five whose eyes bulged with fear, her mouth wide in a silent scream. Last year's Enna glared at Anne with fiery rage imprinted in her narrowed eyes, her lips set in a thin line. Strands of blue streaks in her long blond hair escaped from the bun at the top of her head and fell across her angry face. White knuckles clenched the inside edge of the mirror that held her captive. Anne laughed and twenty-nine year old Enna slammed her fist on the inside of the glass.

Anne turned back to the mirrored wall and pressed on a small chrome disk. The door to a hidden closet sprung open. A small, square folding table leaned against the side. Usually, the table went in the hall, across from the antique mirror. She set it in the center of the room with an embroidered red cloth draped over the top. Anne reached for a new mirror from a stack on the top shelf, identical to those already mounted on the wall. These mirrors were supposed to catch the reflection when she sucked it through the antique mirror, but this year's Enna was already through, sitting in her kitchen. Anne considered how she needed to change the process as she tried the mirror in various spots on the table. Finally, she spread open the hinged stand at the back of the frame and positioned it to face the door. Red candles in cut selenite holders sat on each side. She stepped back when she heard the door handle turn.

"Oh, sorry. I was just looking for the bathroom." Enna pushed the door wide. "What are you doing?"

"Wait!" Anne yelled. She leaped at Enna and slammed her against the door frame.

"Hey!" Enna crumpled to the floor in the hallway.

"You can't come in here." Anne kicked at Enna's leg to push her away and slammed the door behind them.

Enna staggered to her feet and held onto the wall for support. "What's wrong with you?" She rubbed her thigh. "That hurt."

"Stay out of that room," Anne said through clenched teeth. "Just because you're my reflection doesn't mean you have any right to go snooping around my house."

"Fine." Enna sneered. "Can I use the bathroom or do you want me to pee on the floor?"

Anne said nothing, her lips so tight they almost disappeared. She pointed to a door a few feet down the hall. Enna spun around and stomped to the bathroom. She slammed the door behind her. Anne leaned against the wall with her arms crossed on her chest and stood guard. She couldn't trust this one. She needed a little more time to work out the details of how to send her into the mirror.

Enna shut the bathroom door tight behind her and locked it. She looked behind the shower curtain into the tub. Empty. She tugged on the medicine cabinet door. Nothing but bandaids and vitamins. The louvered door to the linen closet opened on its track with a faint shoosh. Towels, bars of soap and a new bottle of shampoo. Like the kitchen, there was nothing of any help to her. She pulled a length of toilet paper from the roll, wadded it up and tossed in the toilet, then flushed. Her reflection looked back at her from the mirror as she washed her hands and smirked. I'm working on it, she mouthed back at herself.

She tried to recall the details of the off-limits room as she dried her hands. Everything had happened so fast and the light was so dim with all those rainbows dancing around. On her left had been a wall of solid mirror, floor to ceiling, but she thought there was an opening to another room. A small table with a couple of candles on it had been in the center of the room. That was all she'd had a chance to see before Anne had tackled her to the floor. She had to get back in that space.

The two woman stared at each other as Enna emerged from the bathroom, their expressions uneasy reflections. Enna stepped forward and closed the gap between them. Anne didn't move.

"So, how are we going to celebrate our birthday?" Enna asked.

57

"Don't worry. I've got an awesome party planned especially for you." Anne smirked. "Now go back in the kitchen and stay there until I tell you otherwise." Her face darkened and her eyes glared at Enna. "Trust me, it'll be a surprise."

"Okay, okay." Enna threw her hands up in surrender. "Geez, I never thought my reflection would be so mean."

"Just go." Anne pointed to the kitchen.

Enna paced her walk down the hall. She glanced at the clouded mirror. For so many years, she thought Anne was just her own reflection, but eight years ago she began to notice subtle differences. She observed Anne at every opportunity, through every reflective surface available—window glass, chrome faucets, brass doorknobs. Everything except that wall of mirrors in that secret room. Finally by chance last year, she watched Anne pull another reflection through the antique mirror. Enna resolved to get through herself and figure out what Anne was up to. It had taken a whole year, but here she was.

Anne's eyes bored into the back of her head. Enna could feel the energy of the other woman's stare as walked into the kitchen. She positioned herself just out of sight around the side of the doorway. After a few seconds, she heard a door open and shut. She peeked around the corner. The hallway was clear.

Without hesitation, Enna opened the pantry door whose back wall had to abut the secret room. Shelves lined both sides of the narrow cupboard. A row of coat hooks spread across the back where a few bags were hung. She pushed them aside and put her ear to the wall. At first, there was nothing. She closed her eyes and concentrated. Finally, she heard a low murmur of unintelligible words. Then there was silence.

Enna pushed her ear harder against the wall and strained to hear. A faint noise then a heavy thump hit against the other side of the wall. Enna startled and banged into a shelf. Three cans crashed to the floor and rolled into the corner. She darted out of the pantry, shut the door behind her and ran toward the sink. When Anne raced into the kitchen a few seconds later, Enna stood at the window looking out at the snow-covered yard.

"I think the sun's trying to come out." Enna opened her eyes wide, tilted her head to the side and turned to Anne with what she hoped was an innocent expression.

"What were you doing in here?" Anne's face was pink and spit flew from her mouth when she yelled.

"Nothing. Just looking out the window."

Anne scurried to the pantry and yanked the door open. "Were you in here?"

"No. Why would I be in there?" Enna blinked and leaned back against the counter. "I did hear a bang a couple minutes ago, but I thought that was you."

Anne faced Enna and studied her face. "I don't know what you're up to, but it won't matter." She slammed the door. "Let's go. The party's about to start."

Anne grabbed Enna's wrist and jerked her forward. She half-dragged her through the kitchen as Enna struggled to stay on her feet.

"Hey! Stop!" Enna held back. "I'm coming. You don't have to pull."

Anne glared at her, but said nothing as she raced into the hallway, Enna's wrist still clutched in her grasp. Enna regained her balance and scuffed after her. When they reached the door to the secret room, Anne stopped short and Enna lurched against the wall. She huffed as she straightened up.

"Stand right here and don't move." Anne shook her finger in Enna's face. "If you think I'm mean now, you really won't like me when I'm angry."

"Fine," Enna said. She stuck out her lower lip. "Some birthday this has turned out to be."

"Oh, you haven't seen anything yet." Anne laughed. She opened the door and slammed it behind her as she scurried into the room.

A glimpse of reflected candle flame showed through the doorway in that brief second before Anne blocked Enna out. A crisp woodsy scent of incense smoke wafted into the hallway. The door had opened wide enough for a peek at the mirrored wall and what was reflected in it. She crossed her arms and waited. She knew exactly what Anne was up to. Enna smirked. This was why she had tricked Anne into bringing her through the mirror and Anne deserved everything she got.

Anne hummed as she placed an elaborately carved crystal wand in front of the mirror on the table. Enna was so gullible, the ritual should be a piece of cake. She'd have to be more careful next year, though. She didn't want to deal with another Enna like this thirty-year-old. Anne stood back and surveyed the table first, then the room around her. Everything was in place and the hook for the new mirror was secured to the wall. She pushed the button and the curtain lowered over the gallery of mirrors. Enna at twenty-nine banged her fist on the glass and Enna at fourteen stuck out her tongue. Anne rolled her eyes. She didn't need any distraction from those Ennas. There was only one she needed to focus on.

"Ok. It's time." Anne opened the door and stood to one side. "Stand right there." She pointed to a spot a foot in front of the table.

Enna moved where Anne indicated and stood with her hands by her side, her fingers clenched. Her body tensed as she looked around the room. It was small. If she stretched out her arms, her fingertips would almost touch the sides. The corners were shadowed in dimmed light from the chandelier. Pale rainbows hung motionless, but their colored pattern on the walls and mirrors made it difficult to focus. Reflected candle flames flitted against the mirrored wall like fireflies caught in a jar and threw jagged shadows across the open space. The fresh fragrance of incense had become the cloying smell of rotted wood. A black drape completely covered the wall to her right. She turned to face Anne who now stood across from her behind the table.

"Welcome to the birthday party." Anne sneered at Enna. "I hope you have a blast."

Anne adjusted the position of the mirror on the table. She reached forward to pick up the crystal wand. With one end held tight in her right hand, she drew a symbol in the air over the mirror.

In an instant, Enna's hand darted out and grabbed the other end of the wand. Anne stumbled forward in surprise but held on tight. Enna pulled the wand—and Anne—around to the front of the table.

"Let go right now!" Anne said through clenched teeth.

"No way!" Enna said, her own face set in determination.

The wand started to vibrate. Waves of energy plucked at Enna's hand. A buzz thrummed through the close air of the room. The rainbows of light swayed as the energy increased. The women tussled with the wand. Anne clutched her left hand tight over her right and yanked. Enna's grip held. Little by little, she dragged Anne closer to the cedar-framed mirror balanced on the table.

"Let go!" Anne screeched. "Grrrrr…"

The two women battled for control. Enna gritted her teeth and pulled just that much harder. She reached out and her extended arm almost reached the glass of the square mirror. Anne grunted and pitched backward. Enna pulled her closer to the table. She sucked in her breath and closed her eyes. She mustered all her strength and jerked on the wand.

Anne lost her balance and fell toward Enna. The energy buzzed louder. Enna stretched toward the table. Her fingertip touched the mirror. A scream pierced the air, instantly cut off by an ear-splitting crack. Enna staggered backwards and landed on her butt on the floor. She still held onto one end of the crystal wand. Her breath came in heavy puffs, the only sound in the stillness of the room. She looked around. Anne was gone.

In the struggle, the mirror had fallen face down on the table. Enna picked it up and saw her own face. Except it wasn't her at all. Anne stared back at her, her eyes wide and her mouth hung open. Her face contorted into a silent scream. Enna laughed. She placed the mirror back on the table. Anne watched her every movement from behind the glass.

Enna stared at the mirrored wall. All the room was reflected in it but she couldn't see herself. She didn't understand, but it explained why she had seen Anne everywhere else in the house but never here in this room. The door to the closet was ajar and she nudged it fully open. It was just for storage, apparently. Extra candles and another table cloth were on one shelf. She stretched on tiptoes to see the shelf above and found another two dozen cedar mirrors like the one that had captured Anne.

Outside the door to the right, a set of keys hung from a slot. Enna turned the switch. A click sounded and then a metallic whirr. She stood with hands on her hips as the black velvet curtain rose slowly. Her breath caught in her throat. Seventeen pairs of eyes stared back at her—her own eyes. Seventeen versions of her own face. She gazed at one after another, then turned the mirror so it faced the gallery. Simultaneously, each Enna noticed Anne trapped behind the glass. Enna at sixteen clapped her hands. Twenty-two year old Enna laughed and waved. Age twenty-seven Enna folded her hands and held them to her lips. Enna at twenty-nine cocked her head and waited. Hope danced across the seventeen faces. Each blond, blue-eyed Enna anticipated her own release.

Anne's face in the mirror exploded in rage. Her face grew red and spit splattered against the inside of the mirror. Some of the Ennas pointed and laughed. Others nodded and huffed in smug agreement. Enna picked up Anne in the mirror and hung it from the hook on the wall, the eighteenth face added to the gallery. All eyes watched to see what Enna would do next. She stepped back to check the mirror, forward again to adjust it a bit to the left. Anne slammed the glass. Enna didn't flinch. Satisfied the frame was straight, she walked to the closet and turned the key in the slot. The curtain descended over the gallery of eighteen faces.

Enna tossed the keys in the air and caught them in her palm. She opened the door and looked back at the half-covered mirrors.

"See you all next year."

Tollenhurst Monastery (Carl Hughes)

Sid Grayson had one bomber of a headache by the time the tourist coach pulled up outside Tollenhurst Monastery – nowadays an upmarket hotel where the coach trippers would be staying for seven nights. Unlike those punters, Sid wouldn't be paying. He had half a dozen commissions lined up from the glossiest mags and Sunday-paper supplements to write about the place and about the tour as a whole. Along with its complimentary tickets, the tour company had promised the vacation of a lifetime. Yeah, well, all his complimentary tickets through the years had come with the same promise, more or less, give or take a cliché or two.

Most of those on the coach were pensioners and, like the majority of their breed, they found it necessary on making new acquaintances to do it at a colossal level of decibels, on and on. Hence Sid's headache. Even the tour guide, Marcel, looked pissed off after being asked a score of times on that long day when the next rest stop would come, as cups of tea were sorely needed and weak bladders required emptying.

Sid had found himself sitting next to an octogenarian called Mimi, who'd told everyone who would listen that 'I refuse to be defined by the number of candles on my birthday cake.' After hearing the old girl recite the same thing ad

65

nauseam, Sid found it as irritating as fleas in a hair shirt.

Tollenhurst Monastery was a great rambling place covered in Virginia creeper, its stained-glass windows reflecting the golden late-summer day that had been drowned in moist heat. Turrets and gables punctured the sky as if reaching for God and finding only futility.

Sid followed the pensioners as they aged off the coach and Marcel caught his eye. The Frenchman said, 'It's been a long but extraordinarily enjoyable day, yes?'

'Hasn't it just?' Sid said ironically. The first requirement of any tour guide was to obtain a degree in drivel from the University of Crapology and Marcel had achieved a Masters.

Marcel and the driver, Harry, began to unload luggage as porters with plastic smiles emerged from the hotel. Meanwhile, the pensioners crawled like woodlice into the lobby. There they queued at the reception desk while Sid asked to see the manager, Mr Ranger.

Mr Ranger proved to be a frog-faced individual with greasy skin and a smarmy way of talking while rubbing his hands over and over as if washing them under an ethereal tap.

'Delighted you could come, Mr Grayson,' the manager said. He was wearing a dinner jacket with a frilly shirt front, which Sid thought incongruous without a five-piece chamber orchestra and dim lights as backing. 'I've arranged for you to have one of our best rooms.'

'Thank you,' Sid said.

'And you will of course write about us kindly?'

'I'll take as I find,' Sid said.

'Oh, of course, naturally. I didn't mean to suggest that you would flatter us without good cause.' The manager laughed, sounding like wheezy bellows. 'And of course my staff and I will always be available to make your stay as comfortable as you could desire. If you require anything, you have only to ask.'

Sid cast a brief glance around the lavish lobby with its chandeliers and glittering mirrors. 'You can start by telling me something of the hotel's history,' he said.

'A fascinating history it is.' Mr Ranger took Sid's arm and guided him into a sheltered spot away from the coughing and phlegmy pensioners. 'Tollenhurst Monastery was founded in the fourteenth century but it fell into disuse in the sixteen hundreds when all the monks were disgraced as they began to die due to syphilis.' He looked tragic, as if the monks had been family members who'd abused his hospitality. 'They indulged in sex, you see,' he added sotto voce, as if he thought Sid would think syphilis might be nothing more than an airborne virus. 'After that the monastery became the country home of Priscilla, Duchess of Darnley, who found herself trapped in an unhappy marriage with the abusive and womanising Duke of Darnley at Cashmore Hall. The Duchess left him to his whores and retreated to Tollenhurst Monastery where she involved herself in what were considered to be unladylike pursuits such as shooting and hunting.'

'She sounds quite a girl,' Sid said.

Mr Ranger looked as startled as if he'd just discovered a lost civilisation. After a moment, his frog face somehow summoning a mournful expression, he said, 'One day Her Grace was killed while out hunting and it's now said her ghost haunts the monastery.' He smiled. 'However, no one alive claims to have encountered the ghost. I certainly haven't. It wouldn't be good for my angina.'

'What happened after the Duchess kicked her regal bucket?' Sid asked.

Mr Ranger looked disconcerted all over again. Then, hands working greasily overtime, he said, 'The monastery became a gentlemen's club and is now, as you see, a five-star hotel that caters for casual visitors, conferences and also coach parties such as yours.'

'Well, I hope I sleep well and won't be disturbed by the late Duchess,' Sid said.

Mr Ranger smiled placatingly. 'I assure you that the ghost is merely a legend but it's always something our guests ask about.' He coughed, looking embarrassed. 'And, I confess, we're glad to exploit the story as a good selling point.'

Sid's room proved to be not much less than a suite, with a cavernous bathroom and a separate sitting area. The carpeting was in rich burgundy and the fittings not so much classy as ostentatious. During his years of travelling, Sid had found that one hotel room or suite tended to blend into all the others but this passed muster so far.

The Queen-sized bed came with a shimmery quilt that looked as if it were as slippery as something found at Aviemore in winter but it proved to be deep and cosseting, if a trifle warm for late summer.

Sid considered spending an hour or so in the bar but the thought of sharing that space with the geriatrics, including Mimi who wouldn't be defined by her birthday candles, acted as a deterrent that his liver would appreciate. So he booted up his laptop computer and began work on the first of his articles. Not having much to say so far, he contented himself with a few platitudes and sketched in a bit of history. By midnight he had just reached the bit about Duchess Priscilla hanging about the place when a hurried rapping sounded at his door.

'Coming!' he called, pushing back his chair from the handily provided writing desk. The rapping continued unabated.

Irritated, he strode across the room as the rapping went on, louder than before. He flung open the door. Outside, the corridor was silent and empty and bathed in gravy-coloured light that created murky shadows all along its length. Sid frowned. Surely no one would have had time to scoot off in the mere second it had taken him to open the door. The air felt greasy and swollen, like something steamed from a putrid carcass. Not five-star ambience for sure.

He wondered grimly if some hotel employee had been assigned the task of playing silly buggers, pretending to be a ghost so he'd give the spooky story prominence in his articles as a lure to the more gullible punters.

'Stupid bugger,' he muttered. 'If it's eerie exaggeration you want, you only have to show me a handful of readies and I'll be happy to oblige.'

After a last glance right and left, he stepped back into his room and closed the door.

He'd moved away only a foot when the rapping came again. Rapid and insistent, an annoyance that set his teeth on edge. 'Clear off, you cretin,' he yelled. It made no difference. The rapping went on and on: noise from the planet of Bedlam.

Incensed, Sid yanked open the door and was greeted again by emptiness and silence. He stepped into the corridor and prowled up and down, peering into the shadows where someone with crap for brains might conceivably have taken cover. But he found nothing.

'Damned if I'll go through this fricking pantomime again,' he said through gritted teeth. His voice sounded as if it had blown a gasket. He hated it when he wasn't in control and on these freebie trips he expected to be pampered. So now he'd tell that frog-faced manager Ranger just what he thought of the man's tricks. And he'd give the hotel a blistering write-up.

He marched along the corridor and down the stairs and approached the reception desk where a clerk with a name tag that could have been an acronym for a new intestinal disorder stood with bugger all to do. Sid planted both fists on the counter and said, 'Get Ranger. I want to talk to him – now.'

The clerk, whose chin looked as if it had been polished with finest French wax, said, 'Who did you ask for, Sir?'

'Ranger. Mr Ranger. The manager.'

The clerk looked nonplussed. 'I'm sorry, Sir, but Mr Ranger passed away more than a year ago.'

'What?'

'I'm afraid so. It was a heart attack. He'd suffered for a long time with angina.'

Sid took a deep breath. 'Listen, Mister, I was talking to your Mr Ranger only a few hours ago, here in the lobby. The frog-faced man in a tuxedo.'

The clerk nodded like one of those toy dogs you used to see in the backs of middle-aged people's cars on Sunday afternoons. 'Yes, that was Mr Ranger, but you're mistaken about having spoken to him tonight. As I say, he died more than a year ago.' He coughed politely and his eyes slid right and left as if watching phantoms perform leapfrog in the ether. 'You are a guest here, of course?'

'I'm a writer. I'm with the coach party that checked in earlier tonight.'

The clerk looked troubled. 'We have no coach parties here at the moment, Sir.'

'Are you doolally or what?'

'Would you mind telling me your name and room number, Sir?'

'Grayson. Sidney Grayson. Room 204.'

The clerk tapped a few computer keys and peered into a screen. 'That room is currently occupied by a Mr and Mrs Proctor. But your name

71

sounds familiar. Will you excuse me while I call the night manager?'

Sid stood, seething, fists clenched, while the unpronounceable object behind the counter picked up an ivory-coloured phone and asked Mr Dulson to come to reception.

A minute later Sid saw to his amazement that Mr Dulson was the clerk who'd checked him in that night. Now, according to this Alice-in-Wonderland world, Dulson had become the night manager.

Sid and Dulson stared at each other, Dulson looking as if he'd encountered a thing scary enough to shrink an enlarged prostate. After a moment he said, 'Mr Grayson! Where on Earth have you been?'

'What d'you mean, where've I been? In my room, of course.'

Dulson had a cherry nose that glowed in the light of the chandeliers and he smelled of some cologne that Sid found as repulsive as corpse's fart. Craning forward as if for a closer look, Dulson said, 'But you vanished from this hotel three years ago and no trace of you was ever found, either here or anywhere else.'

'Christ, d'you take me for an imbecile? Are you hoping I'll write something about this poxy place's spookiness? If so, you've got the wrong guy.'

Dulson and the unpronounceable man exchanged troubled glances and began to mutter to each other about impossibilities and bizarrenesses. Sid found their pantomime as entertaining and convincing as a testament to the wonderful bowel movements of marmosets. After a minute, seething, he said, 'I'm checking out of this place right now

72

and you can tell your Mr Ranger that I'm utterly brassed off with the whole performance.'

Dulson swallowed audibly. 'Please, Mr Grayson, would you mind waiting a moment?'

Before Sid could reply, the night manager vanished into an office at the back and reappeared a minute later clutching half a dozen newspapers and magazines. He spread them on the counter and pointed to their datelines. Sid saw they had evidently all been published three years in the future.

'Right, I've had enough,' he grated. 'I'm returning to my room to pack and then I'm leaving, and God help you when you see the sort of write-up you're going to get from me.' Then, as the two hotel employees stared, he spun on his heel and marched back to his room.

On arrival there he found his electronic key card wouldn't open the door. Fuming, he tried again and again. Then someone opened up from inside. Sid found himself confronted by a squat man with bulging eyes and ears like jug handles. The man was wearing a Japanese-style dressing gown and gaudy pyjamas.

'Who in the name of God are you?' Sid demanded.

The man with the ears frowned and said, 'I could ask you the same question. I think you've got the wrong room, Mister.'

'Like hell I have. This is my room – 204.' Sid jerked a thumb at the numerals screwed into the door.

'That's the right number but my wife and I are staying here. Harold and Marjorie Proctor from Maldon.'

Sid stared at the man for what seemed an eternity before something shifted deep in his psyche. Eventually he muttered an apology and stepped back as Proctor closed the door in his face.

Coldness agitated within Sid's marrow like old linen in a windstorm. No longer could he dismiss the episode as a charade put on purely to scare the bejasus out of him. Something from the Twilight Zone had happened that night – or whatever night it really was.

Standing with his back to the mud-coloured wall, he dragged out his smartphone and called Julie, his partner. The time was after midnight but he was long past caring about courtesies and niceties.

Sounding sleepy, Julie answered after a couple of minutes. Feeling as ravaged and gaunt as a winter tree, Sid said, 'Julie, what year is this?'

'What? What did you say?'

'For Christ's sake, just tell me what year it is.'

'Sid – is that you?'

'Of course it's me. Who did you think it was? Father Christmas?'

'Good God, where've you been for the last three years?'

Clutching the phone as if it were his last and loosest link with reality, stumbling over his words, Sid told her what had happened to him since he'd checked into Tollenhurst Monastery only a handful of hours earlier.

After he finished, Julie said with a bucketful of scorn, 'And you really expect me to swallow that cock-and-bull story? Surely you could have dreamed up something better, you bastard. You've been gallivanting with some floozie, haven't you? And now you think I'll take you back like the well-behaved little girl I'm supposed to be.'

'You've got it all wrong.' Sid's shoulders drooped. He felt utterly weary. Dredging up words, he said, 'We'll discuss it later. I'll be with you as soon as I can. I'm coming home to whatever year this is.'

'Not to this house, you're not. I'm married now to a heavyweight boxer called Alec who'll punch your lights out if you dare show your face. And don't think you can collect your belongings – I chucked them out years ago.'

Sid began to say something but Julie disconnected, a sharp and final click that seemed like the world closing down. Despite the chill still churning inside him, Sid felt sweat coursing down his forehead and stinging his eyes.

Scared, his mind scrambled, wits churning, he found his movements as jerky as those of a palsied marionette as he shifted a few steps along the corridor.

After a minute he slumped on the floor with his back to the wall and drew his knees up as if striving to compress himself out of the space he occupied. Think! he told himself. There has to be a way through this.

The bizarre episode had begun when he left Room 204 and made his way to the reception area.

75

So perhaps, just maybe and please sweet Jesus let it be, perhaps if he returned to the room now occupied by the Proctors, as if he'd never been away, he might possibly return to the past, back where he belonged. Fine, yeah, great – but he couldn't simply turf the Proctors out and shift his own butt back into the place. No, he had to approach this in the right way.

He took a massive breath, stared at the far wall unseeingly, and finally heaved himself upright. Striving to control his movements, not wanting to appear hysterical, he returned to the reception desk. The unpronounceable clerk and Mr Dulson the night manager were still there. They stared in consternation as he approached.

'I want to check back into Room 204,' Sid said. His voice sounded strong enough, not a quaver to disturb its synthetic confidence.

The clerk cocked his head slightly. 'As I said before, that room is already occupied by...'

'Yeah, Mr and Mrs Proctor from Maldon. Can't you move them into another room? A better one maybe?'

Mr Dulson smiled and spread his hands placatingly as if striving to calm a drunkard or a fractious child. Sid felt like booting the man's balls up his anus. Then Mr Dulson said, 'Mr and Mrs Proctor will be checking out first thing this morning. They have to be at the airport by eight o'clock. So, if you'd care to wait just a few hours I'll see the room is cleaned as a matter of urgency and we'll be happy to allocate it to you.'

'Fine. Let's do it. I'll only want the place for an hour or two.'

The clerk coughed. 'Of course, you'll have to pay for an entire day. In advance.'

Sid sneered but produced his wallet from the back pocket of his chinos and handed over his credit card.

The clerk examined it. 'I'm afraid it's two years out of date.'

Sid glared at the man, damning him all the way to Hell. He delved into his wallet again and found he had just enough cash to cover the cost of a day in Room 204.

'Right,' he said, handing it over with a shaking hand. 'Now all I have to do is wait.' Cold cobwebs traced a hideous pattern on his spine.

The room hadn't changed since he left it a few hours ago, or was it three years? Either way, the furnishings looked the same although maybe the duvet was different. He couldn't remember. But okay, now he was in residence, what next? Wait and see, he told himself.

He didn't have to wait long. After ten minutes or so the familiar rapping sounded at his door, on and on, grating on nerves already strung to screaming madness.

Bracing himself, Sid hurried to the door and dragged it open. As expected, the noise ceased instantly and he found the corridor empty, as he'd hoped. Now he'd go down to reception and hope that time had wound back to his own present. It was the longest of shots, like backing a donkey to win the Derby, but he had nothing else to hope for.

Tense, every muscle taut, he paced along the corridor and began to descend the stairs. His footfalls sounded muffled, as dense as water on cotton wool. Which is when something peculiar happened.

From one stair to the next, Sid entered a sort of shimmering chill, clammy and as shocking as a tumblerful of ice thrown in his face. Even the light changed. For a moment it took on an alabaster hue that hurt his retinas. Then, without realising he'd descended further, he found himself on the ground floor.

Only, it wasn't the ground floor as he knew it. The carpeting had been replaced by stone flags while the plush décor and fittings had vanished, exchanged for plain walls of basalt or limestone in a dankness that permeated the frigid air.

Worse, as if looking at something viewed in a mist, he saw several monks in stages of blindness and decay wandering around in the last stages of debauched lives.

Sid fell to his knees and half covered his eyes, screaming, 'Oh good Christ no! No – not this!

Convincing Charlie Burress (Rie Sheridan Rose)

"I tell ya, I seen him."

"Y'r lyin'. No one ever sees him. They might hear him, or see stuff he's moving, but no one ever sees him."

Billy Ingalls balled his fist but remembered what his ma had said about making friends in this new town. He must not get into any fights—and keep the "crazy talk" to a minimum. She couldn't afford to move them again if this didn't work out. So, he counted to ten like she had taught him, and slowly unclenched his fist.

Taking a deep breath, he tried again. "We live in the house next door to the field where it happened, remember? I seen him wandering there last night. You can come see for yourself if'n you want." He crossed his fingers behind his back Ma would be too happy he had made a friend to question Charlie Burress too closely.

The last thing he wanted was Burress as a friend...but proving he wasn't a liar would be worth it. He had never asked to see the ghosts—they just came to him. It had gotten so bad the last place they lived, Ma had moved them here to the back of beyond to start over.

He could have told her it wouldn't work. It never worked. The first ghost he remembered was his grandmother leaning over his cradle when he was six months old. They said no one could remember what happened to them when they were six months old, but Billy did. Until he saw her picture when he was five, he didn't know she was his grandmother. He told his ma how the old lady in the picture used to come sing him to sleep.

Ma had gone all quiet. "Lying is a sin, Billy," she'd said, in a whispery voice—like she feared someone would hear her.

"I'm not lying, Mama. She used to sing me 'Rock a Bye, Baby', but she don't anymore. Guess 'cause I'm not really a baby no more."

Ma's eyes got all teary, and he didn't bring it up again. It wasn't until later he realized Grandma Catherine had died before he was born.

Now he was twelve, he was used to ghosts, but he rarely talked about them anymore. He'd just nod—maybe ask what they needed if he was alone. Try to help them out when he could. Just part of his life.

Occasionally, he'd slip up, like today. With Halloween just around the corner, ghosts proved a frequent topic of conversation. At lunch, the guys had been telling him about Ol' Man Peterson, who used to live next door to the house where he lived now.

"They say he slit the throats of his wife and five kids," said George Fuller, his voice lowered to a hollow groan. "Then he burned down the house with him in it. About five or six years ago."

"Yeah," said Charlie, "and now nothin' will grow there, and every time they try to build somethin' new, there's a fire or somethin' else bad."

80

And then he'd made his mistake. Ma had told him never to talk about ghosts—even though she didn't really believe in them herself. But it was a new school, and he wanted to fit in, and...well, he forgot. Ghosts were so much a part of his life, he forgot sometimes no one else could see them.

"I seen Mr. Peterson last night—if that's the name of the old guy in the lot next door. Seemed like he was looking for something." It had just slipped out between bites of his sandwich.

George had laughed it off. He obviously thought Billy was joking. But Charlie wouldn't let it go. He kept riding Billy about it for the rest of the day. Now, school had let out, and the weekend loomed.

And he'd just invited Charlie Burress to come and ghost-watch with him. Ma would have a cow.

"I just might take you up on that, Boolly," Charlie said with a smirk.

Billy groaned to himself. He'd just gotten his nickname for this school. From now on, he'd be "Boolly, the boy who sees ghosts."

He sighed.

"My ma won't be home until eight or nine, but she won't care if you come over."

Charlie's eyes lit up. "You mean you have the house to yourself between now and then? Hot damn, boy! Your mom got any liquor?"

Billy frowned. "Maybe. I dunno. Why?"

"Whole lot easier to see ghosts when y'r buzzed, boyo!"

He started to tell Charlie he didn't need any help to see ghosts, but decided to shut up while he was ahead.

"I'll be at your house in half an hour," Charlie said, punching his shoulder. "This is gonna be fun!"

Somehow, Billy didn't think so—but he held his tongue. The sad man next door probably wouldn't even come out tonight. He didn't all the time. Billy had only seen him a handful of times, wandering back and forth through the dirt lot next door. Grass grew in spotty patches around the fringes of it, but only bare dirt remained in the center, with ash-covered bricks here and there where they had knocked down the shell of the house. The old man—well, he looked like he might not be much older than Dad, to tell the truth—just wandered back and forth across the lot, wringing his hands and moaning, like he was searching for something he had lost. Kinda sad.

"Sure," he answered automatically, shouldering his backpack, and stepping onto the bus.

When he got home, he did a swift look through his room to make sure nothing embarrassing lay out—like his teddy or the Star Wars Pajamas Aunt June sent last Christmas. Reassured the bedroom looked like that of a typical twelve-year-old boy...a little messy, but no kid junk...he went downstairs to call his ma.

"Lindon House, Barbara Ingalls speaking. How may I direct your call?"

"Ma, it's me. I know I'm not supposed to call you at work unless it's an emergency, but I wanted to let you know I'm having a friend over to spend the night." A tiny white lie…but it would make her feel better.

"Breathe, Billy," she said, with a little laugh. "That's fine. Will you boys be all right by yourselves until I get home? I may be late tonight."

"Ma," he answered, in the pained tone only twelve-year-old boys have mastered, "we'll be fine. We aren't babies."

"True enough. All right then. Behave yourselves, and I'll be home as soon as possible."

"Okay, Ma."

The doorbell rang.

"Charlie's here. Gotta go."

"Have fun. I love you."

"I love you, Ma."

He hung up as a barrage of knocks replaced the ring of the doorbell. By the time he crossed the living room, yells had joined the knocks. "C'mon, dude! Let me in! The beer's getting hot!"

Billy sighed deeply and pasted a smile on his face before he opened the door. He'd planned on a quiet evening at home reading, but this might be better in the long run. If he cultivated Charlie Burress as a friend, he'd be well on his way to fitting in at this school. Next time, he'd invite George too, and he'd be golden.

Throwing open the door, he greeted his guest. "Hey, Charlie. Sorry to take so long getting to the door. Was on the phone with my ma."

Charlie thrust a six-pack of cans at him. "Stick these in the freezer for ten minutes. That'll cool 'em down all right."

Billy looked down at the beer in his hands with misgiving. "I don't think Ma will like this."

"So don't tell her. You said she'd be late, right? We'll drink 'em fast and toss the cans in the lot next door."

"I—"

"You aren't gonna wuss out on me now, are ya?"

Billy shook his head and led the way to the kitchen, sticking the six-pack into the freezer and setting the timer on the microwave for ten minutes.

"Nice place ya got here," Charlie murmured, studying the neat kitchen, then wandering out into the living room. "Just you and your mom here?" He picked up one of Ma's figurines from the display case near the sliding door to the backyard.

"Yeah. Could you put that down, please? Ma'll kill me if any of those get broken."

Charlie raised an eyebrow but set it back where it belonged. "What do you do for fun around here? This place is way out on the edge of nowhere."

"I'm twelve," Billy said dryly. "I read and watch TV. What did you expect?"

Charlie shrugged. "Play in those woods behind the house. Goof off with fireworks..." He turned to Billy with a leer and a rude gesture. "Jerk one off in your bedroom."

This is not going well, Billy thought with a gulp. The beeper going off in the kitchen saved him the need to reply. "Beer's cold," he announced unnecessarily, darting to the kitchen.

Charlie strolled after him. "I was just funnin', Boolly. I know y'r a good little Mama's boy. It's part of your charm."

Billy grabbed the beer out of the freezer as if the cans were white-hot instead of ice cold and put it on the counter. "Want a glass?"

"Nah. Glasses are for sissies."

Billy pulled his hand down from the glass he'd been about to lift out of the cabinet. "Uh, right."

Charlie popped the top on a can with a loud hiss. "Here. This'll put hair on your chest."

Billy really didn't want hair on his chest, but he took the can and cautiously managed a sip. He almost spat it out again, but forced himself to swallow. "Good," he murmured, as Charlie opened another can.

"Damn right, good. This is the best!" He chugged half the can and then belched loudly. "Ah! That really hits the spot."

Billy began to regret ever hatching this stupid plan. Did he really need a friend like Charlie? No matter how popular he was.

"So, c'mon, dude. Grab the rest of the beer, and let's go ghost-hunting." Charlie headed for the sliding door like he owned the place.

Billy slipped his fingers through the empty rings on the six-pack yoke and followed Charlie out into the backyard. It felt chilly outside this late in October, and he shivered, debating whether he should grab a jacket. Charlie was in shirtsleeves though, and that decided him.

"I remember the house a little," Charlie murmured, taking a swig of beer, and then pitching his can into the empty lot. "It was two-story, like yours, but more rundown, y'know. Straggly bushes, no paint…"

Billy could almost see it in his head.

"My friend Morty used to live in your house. We spent a lot of time playin' with Stevie Peterson. He was a nice guy. Gimmee another beer."

Billy handed over the remaining cans with alacrity, pretending to take another swig from his own can as he did so. He was darn sure not taking another one.

Charlie popped the top and took a swig. "Funny, I'm startin' to remember all kinds of things now. How pretty Stevie's big sister Karen was—the kinda girl you dream of growin' up to marry. The twins were barely walkin' and Jason was just home from school for the summer. He was way older— maybe from a different marriage. He and Karen were close in age, and then the three younger ones. Their mom always had a plate of cookies coolin' in the kitchen—cocoa in the winter, lemonade in the summer. Mr. Peterson seemed nice enough. He called me Chuckles and gave me a nickel every time he saw me." He gulped down the rest of the beer and threw the can as far as he could.

Billy heard the can thunk into a tree trunk on the other side of the lot. Then, as if conjured by the conversation, Mr. Peterson's ghostly form materialized where the rear of the house must have been, and he moved forward, wringing his hands as he searched the lot in a zig-zag pattern.

Now he was outside instead of watching from his bedroom window, Billy could hear the ghost as well as see him. Low moans, punctuated now and then by a call of "Stevie! Stevie, where are you?"

Charlie was staring at him. "What's wrong with you, dude? You're white as a sheet."

"Don't you see him? He's right over there." Billy pointed a shaking finger.

Charlie whirled. "There's no one there! I knew you were nuts."

"Can't you hear him? He's calling for Stevie. That's what he's looking for."

Charlie's face grew still. "He's what?"

Billy concentrated hard. The ghostly figure had wandered across the lot for the moment, flickering between the fringes of the trees. "He's saying, 'Stevie! Stevie, where are you?' over and over again."

Charlie plopped to the ground, cracking open another beer. "It was the Fourth of July, y'know. The night the house burned. I remember now. Me and Morty and Stevie were playing with bottle rockets. We weren't supposed to, but we were. And it was late. Prolly close to midnight. We were six. Should have been in bed. But we were sitting over there at the edge of the woods, shooting off bottle rockets."

The ghost had made his way over to their side of the lot again. He was much clearer now. His face creased with worry, and he raised his hands to his mouth like a funnel and bellowed, "Stevie! Come inside now! It's way past your bedtime!"

Charlie jumped up, staring toward the apparition.

"Did you hear him?" Billy asked eagerly. "Can you see him?"

Charlie shook his head. "I thought—no. I don't hear nothin'."

The ghost stiffened, his eyes tracking an arc overhead, and then spun toward the space where his house had been. A look of terror flashed across his face, and he sprinted across the lot. When he got to where the back porch would have been, he put an arm up, as if to protect his face, charged into the house, and was gone.

Billy sank to the ground beside Charlie. "He didn't kill his family, did he?" he asked softly.

Charlie shook his head, tears running down his cheeks. "We didn't mean to." The words were soft, the tone a small child's. "It was the last one. A skyrocket had gotten mixed in somehow. We saved it till the end, so excited to see what it would do. Stevie held the can, and I lit it. But...something happened. I don't know if he dropped it, or what, but the rocket didn't go up, like it was supposed to. It flew toward the house. I-I don't remember Mr. Peterson being outside, but he might have been. I didn't remember any of this till now." He sobbed like a child now, and Billy felt a deep sympathy for the pain he must be feeling. "The rocket hit the house and exploded. It had been a dry summer, and—like I said—the house was rundown. It went up like a torch."

"What happened to Stevie?"

"Morty and I tried to hold him, but he squirmed free and ran toward the house. Last I saw of him, he ran inside." Charlie raised the can in his hand to his lips, then stopped dead and threw it away from him. Beer sprayed out in an arc, perfuming the air with the scent of malt and hops. Jumping to his feet, he lobbed the remaining cans, one after another.

"No more of this shit!" he grunted. "I need to take responsibility, don't I?"

Billy stood and put a hand on Charlie's shoulder. "You were just a little kid, Charlie. It was so bad you completely suppressed it all these years. I guess you could tell someone if you wanted to, but what good would it do? What happened to Morty?"

"He moved before school that year. I don't know for sure what happened to him, but I do remember we didn't play together anymore."

Billy whispered, "It wasn't your fault, Charlie. It was an accident. A bad one, but you guys were just babies. I think you've punished yourself enough."

Charlie turned haunted eyes to face him squarely. "And you could see what happened?" he murmured.

"Some of it. Mr. Peterson ran into the burning house—I guess to try and save his family. Stevie ran in after." Billy met Charlie's stare. "It isn't cool people think he killed them, Charlie. Not when he died trying to save them."

"What can we do about it?"

Billy sighed. "I dunno. We're just kids. I bet the bodies burned up to a crisp. I wonder how the murder story even started…"

"I honestly don't know that," Charlie said with a shrug, already sounding older and wiser than the boisterous boy who had called him Boolly. "Could have been someone who didn't like Mr. Peterson—who wanted to ruin his reputation or something?"

"Maybe."

Billy thought long and hard. "There must be something we can do about it. My ma may know."

"Y'r gonna tell your mom? Won't she freak out?"

"She already knows I see ghosts."

"My mom would freak. Y'r really lucky, Billy."

Billy looked across to the empty lot, where the ghost of Mr. Peterson stood, lifting Stevie above his head, then swooping him down into a crushing hug. The ghosts looked over at the boys and waved before fading away completely.

"Did you see that?" Charlie breathed. "Did you see that?"

Billy laughed. "Yeah, bud. I saw it."

"And you see stuff like that all the time?"

"Since I was a baby."

"I don't envy you, bro—but that was amazing."

"Yeah, it's nice when there's a happy ending, isn't it?" Billy clapped Charlie on the shoulder. "Let's go play a game."

As they walked back into the house, Billy sneaked a look at the lot next door. He had a feeling he'd seen the last of Mr. Peterson.

A Lick of Paint (Stephen Lang)

The taxi followed the tree-lined lane that led away from the village. The low winter sun peeked through the branches, casting long finger-like shadows that seemed to point the way. The driver told me the cottage was the easiest of places to find.

I'd arranged to meet the owner - a Mr Packer - at the property. I saw him by the gate as the taxi drew up, hands in pockets as he surveyed the cottage, perhaps trying to decide if it really would suit my needs. He had a full head of white hair, but his rosy cheeks boasted an air of youth, and his attire complemented this with his casual dress of tracksuit and trainers.

We shook hands after I'd paid the driver.

"Mr Whittington," he said, "I'm Ted Packer. You found it okay, then?"

"Yes," I replied, "couldn't be easier."

Packer stifled a cough as he unlocked the front door. The living room smelt musty when we entered; the place no doubt unaired for a long time. Packer pulled the curtains apart with a flourish, although it made little difference. The trees that towered outside allowed for scarce light, and the sudden movement caused a small cloud of dust to engulf us.

"Here we are," he said. "I told you not to build your hopes up, didn't I?"

He had indeed, although I'd only skim-read Packer's emails. The cottage interior was the same as in his photographs; dark wainscoting panelled the lower walls, and a narrow dining table and two chairs provided sparse furnishing. Packer gestured towards a hearth with copious wood stacked on either side.

"There's plenty for you to burn," he said. "Long winter nights and all that."

"Nothing better than an open fire," I replied.

I handed him the two hundred pounds. It wasn't much in the way of three weeks' rent, but Packer had repeatedly stressed the point to me about not expecting too much. He wet the end of his finger with the tip of his tongue before counting the notes.

"What is it you do again, Mr Whittington?"

"I'm a writer," I replied.

He sniffed.

"A writer."

"Yes. I need somewhere quiet to work to complete the editing of a manuscript. Hence…"

"The cottage is sound," said Packer. I realised he was the sort who had a habit of interrupting. "Safe and sound," he continued. "I make sure of that. It might not look too pretty, but there's nothing a lick of paint won't remedy. But that's not for you to worry about."

"I'm sure…"

"I know the place is old and lacking TLC, but it has bags of charm. Nobody can deny that. I'll pop by in a day or two to see if you've settled in. If you'd like to note anything missing in the meantime that you might need?"

"I'm sure I'll be comfortable."

"Just one thing. Keep the front door closed. I know you will, as it's cold out there. But please keep it closed. Pesky cats like to sneak in, and the buggers are hard to get out. I can't stand the bloody things."

"I guess I'm agnostic towards them," I said.

Packer frowned, not following what I'd said. He pocketed the money and shook my hand again before showing himself out. I'd forgotten to ask him for essential information, such as the location of the fuse box and the workings of the boiler, but it didn't matter too much, and I was sure there'd be a detailed email in my inbox that I'd overlooked. Besides, I'd been keen for him to go so I could start work.

I took my bags up the narrow stairs to the bedroom. Comfortable. It was better than that. The cottage was perfect.

***

Although the wood was damp, I soon had a fire going. I warmed myself in front of the flames before turning on my laptop.

I enjoyed the job of editing - all the cutting, revising, and improving. I was shaping a year's work. It just took a long time, hence my decision to rent a property in a remote part of the country. I needed quiet and isolation away from the distractions of London. Three weeks wasn't long in the scheme of things. My family would barely miss me.

The flames cracked and sputtered in the hearth, and darkness soon fell as I absorbed myself in my work. The outline of the trees outside merged with the black of night, the only light the blaze of the fire and the bright screen of my laptop. I'd made good progress and earned myself a cigarette break.

I knew I didn't need to go outside to smoke. Packer wouldn't find out, and I was sure he wouldn't care if he did. It was just habit. I'd become conditioned to smoking in the open air. I also wanted to step into the garden for a few minutes to experience the dead of night.

But all wasn't quiet outside. I could hear a tinkling sound, a soft ringing noting my presence. I found a series of bells fastened to the overgrown bushes at the front of the cottage. The row of tiny tin chimes was like something from a toy shop, tied to the deadheads of the hydrangeas with a fine thread.

The tinkling had now stopped. Wondering if I'd imagined it, I pulled at the thread to test the bells. They tinkled again.

***

Settling back down to my work, I noticed the chipped black paint on the wainscoting had begun to peel away in hard flakes. I reasoned the cottage must have been last decorated decades ago. On closer inspection, I realised the colour of the paint was dark red rather than black. I ran my hand over a section, and it caught against something.

"Damn!"

I'd nicked a finger, and the end of a jagged shard of paint had embedded itself under the nail. It held firm like a splinter when I tried to pull it out. A pinprick of blood matched the dark red colour.

I went through to the kitchen. The sideboard drawers contained cutlery mixed with various other odds and ends. A measuring tape. A paintbrush, its black bristles long-hardened and stiff. A knife.

I slid the end of the blade under my fingernail and levered the splinter out. It glistened wet with my blood. I wrapped my finger in a tea towel.

My accidental handiwork had exposed a yellow-white beneath the dark red on the wainscoting where I'd dislodged the shard of paint. The shape formed a long vertical slit, narrow like the pupil of a cat's eye.

I continued scratching away with the knife. I widened the pupil - dilating it - to allow my imaginary cat to see better in the dark. Did the altered shape indicate excitement in the creature? Had I fashioned a glowing eye that reflected in the light from the hearth?

No, I hadn't.

I scraped at the eye until it was gone. My actions were all so foolish I almost laughed out loud. I'd made no such thing as an eye on the wainscoting.

But when I looked again, the hole in the paint now resembled the shape of a head.

I put down the knife.

***

I surveyed the front of the cottage in the morning as Packer had done the afternoon before. It did look - as he had put it - sound. The brickwork was in good order, and the structure boasted a tall, solid chimney as if its sole purpose was to keep my fire going.

The tinkling this time was louder and came from a different part of the garden. I found more bells tied to the plants and shrubbery on the other side of the cottage. Something had set them off, some intruder trying a different path, but the additional bells had thwarted them.

I followed the tree-lined lane to the village, stooping under the branches and sidestepping their scratchy ends. I came to find a hardware store called the Old Market and a corner Spar shop.

A sign above the counter greeted my entrance.

BEWARE OF THE CAT

I assumed it was a private joke, at least a welcome change to the ubiquitous KEEP CALM AND CARRY ON.

I gathered some cooked meats, fish, eggs and bacon. I found a reasonable cucumber, broccoli, carrots and a bottle of Merlot. I had enough to make a few rudimentary meals.

I eavesdropped on the conversation between the assistant at the till and a customer. They were preoccupied with the weather, discussing how a storm had come and gone and was due to return. I handed the assistant my basket when they'd finished.

"Do you need a bag?" he asked, half-heartedly reaching for a plastic carrier. The Spar logo decorated the breast of his black t-shirt, and dense green tattoos covered his arms.

I shook my head, indicating the rucksack on my shoulder.

"That one has a nice taste," he said.

The assistant nodded approvingly at the Merlot. He wet the end of his finger with his tongue before wrapping the bottle in white paper.

"Oh," he said as I put it in my rucksack.

My finger was still bleeding, and a smear of red had discoloured the white paper.

***

I found a new string of bells tied to the garden gate. I rushed inside to examine the wainscoting as if I had to prove a connection.

The shape was indeed in the form of a head, but human, animal or other, I couldn't determine. Shards covered the carpet where I'd hacked away the paint. I put the largest in my pocket before preparing my evening meal.

The rain lashed against the windows. As predicted in the corner Spar shop, the weather had taken a turn for the worst. But despite the storm, I was sure I could still hear the bells outside.

Consuming the wine caused me to get up in the night. I used the toilet without turning on the light, with mixed success. But I knew the light would tempt me to resume my work downstairs.

My work on the wainscoting.

***

I followed the tree-lined lane to the village in the morning. The bell above the door of the Old Market chimed to announce my entrance.

The hardware store was full of clutter. I stepped around plastic buckets that stood in other buckets, stacked like Russian dolls. I dodged mops and brooms of varying lengths that hung from the ceiling.

The proprietor sat in front of the sign on the counter as if it provided some safety for her.

BEWARE OF THE CAT

She huddled up to a portable radiator, her face so pale, looking like she waited for the nearby source of heat to help pump her blood for her. She rubbed her hands together as she narrowed her eyes at me.

"Yes?"

"I … yes. I'm looking for some paint."

"What kind of paint?" she asked.

"A tin of gloss paint. Dark red. Very dark. Almost black, but not quite. Here."

I took the shard from my pocket and placed it on the counter.

"Gloss?" she said. "I'll have to check."

She picked up a brochure from the counter, wet the end of her finger with the tip of her tongue and turned over a page.

"Hmm."

She wet her finger again and turned another page.

"Berry Red," she said. "This one." She moved the brochure so I could see it. "Looks the closest match. I'll have to order it in. Will a litre tin be enough for you?"

"A litre? Er, yes. I suppose. Yes, that will be fine."

"I'll get the lad to pop it round for you," she said as she closed the brochure. "Probably tomorrow."

"I'm staying in a place on the lane that leads away from the village." I pointed vaguely in the direction of the cottage. "I'll give you the address."

She shook her head.

"There's no need, Mr Whittington."

She knew of me. I guessed she also knew Ted Packer, and I'd been subject to local gossip. Visitors must be a rarity, especially in the winter, and visitors were much more interesting than the weather. There was now a risk she might tell Packer about the paint. But a lick of paint was what the cottage so desperately needed.

I paid for the tin of Berry Red, a small paintbrush and a pack of assorted sandpaper sheets.

"Thanks," I said. "I'll look out for - for the lad."

I turned to navigate my way out of the shop.

"Mr Whittington?"

"Yes?"

"Don't forget your sample."

I picked up the shard and slipped it into my pocket.

"You ought to put something on that," she said.

My wound had started to bleed again. Without thinking, I put the tip of my finger in my mouth and sucked it.

***

The bells had further multiplied. I found them strung along the top of the fence surrounding the cottage, arranged like Christmas decorations. No, not quite that, as I knew the bells were a deterrent. They functioned to stave off the unwelcome - and how they criss-crossed along the fence gave the impression of barbed wire.

I scratched away with the knife. I couldn't bear to look at the head shape any longer. I filled the hearth with wood so the light from the fire would intensify my work. I intended to carve out a featureless hole until my delivery of Berry Red allowed me to set about repainting the wainscoting.

The heat soon grew unbearable. I wiped the dripping sweat from my forehead. But it wasn't sweat. Blood was all over my hands and face. I didn't know how long it had been there. And from one tiny cut? No wonder the woman in the Old Market had eyed me so suspiciously. I dried my face with the tea towel.

I'd neglected my editing with my ridiculous preoccupation with the wainscoting. I'd have a brief cigarette break before getting back to work.

But what was work? The most important work? What - exactly - would that be?

I heard a tinkling sound at the side - no - at the back of the cottage when I was outside. I tripped across more bells as I tried to find the source of the disturbance. All to no avail. It was impossible to move in any direction without setting off a cacophony of bells.

**

The shape on the wainscoting had changed. Evolved, you might say.

It was now more symmetrical, with triangular ears framing the top of the head. I could also make out two eyes. Hairline scratches spread out from both sides of the face to form white whiskers.

Yes, it had a face.

I dropped the knife when I heard the knocking at the front door. There'd been no prior warning from the bells. Who was this? How had they managed to reach the cottage so silently?

It had to be Ted Packer. He would know the quietest way. I'd ask him the purpose of the bells and get to the bottom of it all. But why was he calling so late?

A young man stood on the path outside, his pale face obscured by the hood of his raincoat. Its tip reached down as far as the end of his nose.

"Mr Whittington?"

He held up a small tin of paint. I realised it must be the lad from the Old Market. The tin was surprisingly diminutive for a litre. I knew I should have ordered more.

"How did you not disturb the bells?" I asked. "Which way did you come?"

He looked behind him as if he'd missed something. I followed his line of vision. The bell-covered gate at the end of the path was closed.

"What are you on about?" he said. "What bells?"

I took hold of the lad's arm.

"The bells! Can't you see them? How did you not disturb the bells? Tell me!"

He pulled away from me and took a step back. The lad put the tin of paint down, turned and hurried off.

"Hey," I said. "Wait!"

But he didn't wait, again managing to open and close the gate silently behind him as he left. Seconds later, he was gone.

I locked the front door. I prised open the lid of the tin with the knife.

The face on the wainscoting was now more prominent, resembling a cat with long white whiskers. It watched me with its glowing eyes.

I didn't have nearly enough paint, but I would make a start by covering the cat's face.

I picked up the pack of sandpaper. But before I could open it, a rough tongue ran across the tips of my fingers.

I'd felt such a tongue before. I was agnostic to the creatures, at least until now.

The tongue licked it clean.

The blood, I mean.

My blood. It had tasted my blood.

"No," I said. "No."

The cottage was sound. Ted Packer had said so. It lacked TLC, but it was safe and sound.

Or was it?

As the taxi driver had told me, it was the easiest of places to find.

I hurried up the narrow stairs and lay down on the bed.

I'd let it in when I opened the door to the lad from the Old Market. The lad bypassed the bells. Whatever Packer had set up to keep me safe - whatever strange thing he had done with the bells - I'd ruined it by ordering the paint. Packer had asked me to make a note of anything I needed. He'd told me to keep the door closed.

I'd failed at that.

The lad had allowed its passage.

I googled "human foods that cats enjoy" on my phone.

Cooked meats. Fish. Eggs and bacon. Cucumber. Broccoli. Carrots.

"No," I said. "No."

There'd be a simple solution. I'd go downstairs and forget about the paint. I'd open the door to let - it - out, return to the Old Market in the morning and ask the proprietor to call Packer. We'd work this all out. I'd explain the importance of my work.

My work? What was that?

I had something - something to shape. That was it. I needed to go downstairs to examine the wainscoting.

The rough tongue licked my cheek. Rough like sandpaper.

My blood, licking it clean.

"No," I said. "No."

But I knew the tongue wouldn't stop. It liked the taste too much.

The Darker Season (Phil Thomas)

Not a soul could be seen. The beaches were empty. The welcoming rows of storefronts were dark. The amusement rides were silent. Luke and his cousin Jonathan stood at the base of the Giant Ferris Wheel on Morey's pier and marveled at its stature.

One of the last relics of its time, its surroundings had been replaced long ago by flashier rides and attractions. Every few moments, the circular metal structure creaked and swayed, reminding them of its enormous presence.

It had been many ocean tides since he'd stepped foot on Wildwood's boardwalk. The last time proved itself too difficult, and it took six long years for him to return comfortably. He decided to give it another attempt when his cousin, Jonathan, asked to accompany him to the Jersey shore on a cold January weekend. Jonathan had grown up in the Midwest, having no access to the beaches or ocean, so Luke felt obligated to chaperone his cousin's first visit.

They checked into The Avalon Motel—a place he and his family stayed when he was growing up. After they located their room, the first one next to the bottom-floor office, they unpacked and locked up before heading to the boardwalk. Luke received an alert on his phone about an approaching snowstorm as they made their way from their temporary residence to Morey's Pier.

As they stood at the base of the Giant Ferris Wheel, listening to the gentle creaks, the first snowflakes began to fall. "It's too bad we can't ride it," Jonathan said, admiring its circular height.

"It's January," Luke countered. "I don't think either one of us wants to be up there right now." They left the Ferris wheel behind and moved past the bumper cars and Sea Serpent and The Musik Express—with a k—approaching the main boardwalk.

Conditions escalated, and they agreed to head back to the motel to get warm. But as they exited the pier through a wall of flurries, Luke noticed a giant advertising billboard overhead that he'd not seen since he was a child. A cartoonish picture of Count Dracula and a giant bat rested between the forgotten words: Now better than ever, Castle Dracula.

"It can't be," Luke said, staring at the impossible, experiencing a spasm of denial. After he shook the uneasiness, they proceeded to a section of the boardwalk formally known as Nickels' Midway Pier. The pleasant aroma of popcorn and hotdogs began to ride the gusty winds, and the distant sounds of organ music crept through.

Luke recognized the music to be Bach's Toccata and Fugue. It was Dracula's theme. And appropriate for this occasion because once the cousins reached the end of the pier, the same castle advertised on the billboard somehow welcomed them. Luke felt his energy plummet, and his vision pinpricked when he realized that Dracula's Castle had rebuilt itself to its original grandeur.

Its blood-tinted windows glared back at them as they approached the entryway to the castle. And the raised drawbridge echoed a release, crashing just inches from where they stood.

"Whoa," Jonathan said. "Look at that!" But Luke didn't share his cousin's enthusiasm, especially when the statue of the infamous vampire rolled out on wheels and stopped on the right-side balcony. The small light bulbs in its eyes flashed green and red while its arms stretched out, turning and pointing in Luke's direction.

"That's odd," Jonathan added. "Does this operate all winter long?" Since this was Jonathan's first trip to Wildwood, he wouldn't have known the difference, but Luke had visited the coastal resort every summer with his parents and siblings since he was five years old. And he knew that this was not only strange—but also impossible.

The castle had burned to the ground in the early morning hours of January 16th, 2002. Nothing was left. But here it was, existing on the anniversary of its demise, eighteen years later.

What did it want?

"Step right this way," a smooth voice whispered from somewhere. Luke craned his neck to the drawbridge, just as a nebulous figure in a black hooded robe and skeletal face-makeup materialized from the castle's entrance and made its way across the bridge. The grim reaper apparition seemingly glided on air, carrying a realistic-looking scythe.

Jonathan smiled and clapped Luke on the shoulder. "Hell yeah," he said. "We can kill some time until the storm passes." Luke shook his head and pulled Jonathan aside. He took a deep breath and whispered, "This building shouldn't be here."

Jonathan raised an eyebrow and glanced up at the castle. "I don't know what that's supposed to mean, but here it is."

"It means that the structure burned down almost twenty years ago."

Jonathan looked down at his cousin, and the expression on his face told Luke that he was losing his mind. "So, this is a ghost castle," Jonathan continued. "Is that what you're saying?"

Luke pondered the question for a moment, realizing any response would make him sound crazy. "Yes, that's what I'm saying," he replied, looking deflated. "There was nothing left."

"Luke," Jonathan spoke up, "a torched castle can't just reappear. What you're claiming is impossible. I'm going in. You can either wait here or—"

"Gentleman," the grim reaper interrupted, "the time is now."

Jonathan flipped his hood up to curb the numbing sensation on his face and started toward the apparition.

Fate had dealt its ugly hand, and Luke reluctantly followed, seeing no other choice. Not only was he frightened, but a part of him was also curious. He had buried a secret long ago. A secret that he'd kept hidden for almost twenty years.

A range of childhood memories returned to Luke while they followed the figure across the bridge and into the first darkened room of the castle where a portrait of Count Dracula hung. His eyes were still, but they appeared to watch Luke wherever he went.

The ghostly tour guide marveled at the portrait as if it were a showroom car display. He explained to Luke and Jonathan how the vampire had been unhappy with the current state of his castle. How boardwalk visitors now walk by like it no longer exists, ignoring it altogether.

The specter appeared to only look at Luke when it spoke, burrowing its kill-shot eyes into his. "The master is planning something big, I can assure you," was the last thing he said before leading his guests out of the circular room and down a long hallway. It had been decorated to resemble a medieval castle, complete with suits of armor lined along the hallway passages, battle axes on the walls, and hanging chandeliers with dancing flames and phantom groans that lamented through the castle hallways. It was just like Luke remembered. The interior's past had come alive, reverting to the way it had been.

At the end of the corridor was a skeleton sitting on a throne between two suits of armor, stomping its feet. It was obviously fake, probably constructed of plaster and paste. But after the group passed and turned left, Luke heard its stomping pattern shift, as if it were standing and walking towards them. He decided not to check.

When they arrived at the halfway point, Luke encountered the same dark passageway that resulted in a panic attack as a young child, prompting his father to escort him out through the emergency exit.

In its smooth voice, the figure pointed at Luke and said, "Many a man and child have been reduced to tears at the sights and sounds of what we've experienced thus far. Isn't that correct?" Luke felt white shock run through his body. He didn't know how the guide could possibly know a thing about him.

The reaper only answered Jonathan's questions, and anytime Luke made an inquiry, he simply ignored him and continued with his duties. Uneasiness pressed down on him as they continued deeper into the heart of the castle, and Luke got the sense that he would never leave.

After a few more harrowing rooms—one of which required Luke to climb into Dracula's rudimentary casket so he could experience how the legendary vampire spent his days—they exited via the drawbridge and into the continuing blizzard. Jonathan appeared to be walking on air from the experience, but Luke was just elated to have made it out in one piece.

Just as the cousins were about to emerge onto the boardwalk, the phantom spoke up. "We are not finished with our tour, just yet," it seethed. "I must insist that you accompany me on the castle's underground boat ride. It's just right down there." He motioned to a wooden staircase that descended to a moat where various paddle boats floated, attached to steel underwater tracks. There was no way Luke was about to push his luck a second time. "The master is waiting, just beyond the tunnel," the reaper added.

Luke turned to Jonathan, who simply shrugged his shoulders and said, "Let's do it, cuz. We've already gone this far."

"Thank you for the tour," Luke said to the phantom, "but I think we've already taken up enough of your time. We should get going."

The looming guide stood stock-still, twisting the scythe in his bony hands. "Time is something I have plenty of," it moaned. "I have too much of it, in fact. You must now come with me."

Before Luke knew what happened, the phantom reached out and clutched his wrist with its bone-cold hands, squeezing into his skin until it felt as if his ligaments would tear. He attempted to pull away, but the reaper's grip tightened, twisting and digging.

"Okay," Luke relented, nodding and looking up into the ghoul's blank eyes. "I'll go with you." The figure eased its grasp, allowing him to break free. Jonathan wore a grin, assuming that the reaper had remained in character for effect. Luke knew differently.

He felt it.

He concluded that if he took that ride, he would never make it out. Through thin breaths, he hung back from the phantom and quickly, carefully, explained his most guarded secret to Jonathan as they followed their escort down the stairs and towards the rickety wooden boats.

"Why are you telling me this right now?" Jonathan asked.

"Because I've never told anyone before. I have a feeling that—"

"That's enough talking," the phantom interrupted, turning to them, flipping the switch on the wall, snapping the ride's motors to life. The boats swayed and vibrated on the steel rails, ready to make their departure. "Now enter the vessel."

Jonathan glanced one more time at Luke and attempted to climb aboard. The figure held out a wrinkled palm. "Wait," it moaned with soft-spoken intensity, moving his hand towards Luke, and extending a bony finger. "Only Luke."

"But," Jonathan protested.

"I said, only Luke."

Luke knew that he had never given his name, nor was it ever spoken in the reaper's presence. But he fulfilled his destiny and willingly climbed into the boat, leaving Jonathan to wait by the entrance.

Terror sang in Luke's veins as the motor sputtered, and the reaper guided them down the inky moat, past the lion's head fountains attached to the castle's stone wall. He only turned once to his cousin before the tunnel's darkness consumed them.

Jonathan waited for hours at the castle gates. No Luke. He left the motel door unlocked that night, hoping he'd return. No Luke. He went back the next day, but nothing remained. No castle. No moat. No boat ride. No Luke. He thought about the secret his cousin had told him. At the time, it seemed ludicrous, but now there was no mistaking the truth. Castle Dracula hadn't just accidentally caught fire; it was intentionally burned down by two adolescents. One of the teens responsible was a fifteen-year-old named Luke Briars. Adolescent clemencies only remain for so long before they eventually catch up.

And Jonathan knew that Luke and the castle were together, somewhere.

The Boarders (Phil Thomas)

Journal Entry One:

I'd be dead if they knew I was writing this. I was sixteen years old when I first met the traveling family of four. It was the second week of December, and I was in the process of hanging a holiday wreath on the front window of my mother's recently inherited townhouse when the Isaacs arrived at our doorstep looking for a place to stay until Christmas.

They were a traditional family that appeared to encompass our same values and morals. This was so important to my mother that she didn't even put them through the usual screening process that was required to stay at our boarding house. Maybe it was because they paid upfront for the entire duration of their stay, or perhaps it was because Mr. Isaac reminded her of my deceased father. In any case, we'd already had five boarders staying with us, and the Isaacs filled the final vacancy.

I was able to meet their oldest child, Madeline, on the first night. She was around my age, and I soon realized we had a lot in common. We talked for hours that evening while she graciously helped me decorate the Christmas tree that sat in the center of the small lobby. She was my first crush. I never fell so hard for anyone before or since, and I now owe everything I have to her.

For the next three days, I rushed home after school, heart-pounding, runnels of sweat soaking my shaggy tumbleweed hair, hoping to cross her path in the lobby. But each time I was met with disappointment.

"Why don't you knock on their door?" my mother suggested. "Invite them to eat with us tonight." My mom and I provided a complimentary dinner each night for the guests, which we included in the price of the room. Their family had yet to join us, so I decided to knock on the door to their second-floor residence and invite them.

No answer.

As I sat at the dinner table that night listening to the Christmas carolers outside, I observed something peculiar. I can't believe it took me that long to realize it, and I feel a bit foolish looking back. Three empty chairs sat across from me, intended for our live-in boarders, Mrs. Winter, Mr. Lewis, and Mr. Becker. None of them had missed a meal in over six months, and now all of them were absent. My mom noticed it too, as well as our other two remaining tenants, Miss. McGill and Mr. Brandt.

I usually worked at the front desk in the morning and realized I had not seen Mr. Lewis or Mr. Becker leave for work that day. It was a rare occasion when I didn't have to help Mr. Becker crank his Ford Model T to get it started, but now it made sense.

When I finished eating, I retrieved the brass room keys and knocked on Mrs. Winter's door. The purr of her Tabby Cat followed, along with the beast's incessant scratching of the lower door frame. I don't remember much about the cat, except that it attacked my mother and me on more than one occasion, confusing our legs with scratching posts. I still have the scars to prove it.

Mrs. Winter didn't answer. So next, I tried Mr. Becker's room, then Mr. Lewis. Same result, except their rooms were silent. I wouldn't ordinarily take it upon myself to enter a guest's room without permission, but it felt warranted in that situation. I retraced my steps and tried every doorknob to no avail. The brass key ring I held contained every key to every room in the boarding house. It was the heaviest damned thing and felt like dead concrete. I located the key for room 208 and knocked one last time.

"Mrs. Winter," I called out. I'm coming in." The door creaked open, revealing a menagerie of belongings strewed across the floor: overturned chairs and heaps of clothing and jewelry thrown about—but no Mrs. Winter, only the cat who squinted up at me and purred.

I did the same thing with Mr. Lewis and Mr. Becker's rooms. Both occupants were absent, their rooms ramshackled. I locked the doors and told no one.

Things progressed the next night. Mr. Brandt hadn't shown up, leaving only Miss McGill at the table. Halfway through the meal, the front door opened, and I glimpsed Madeline's incandescent smile as she entered the lobby. She was alone and later explained to me that she had gone for a walk to clear her head. I'd never been so happy to see someone in my life.

We talked for about an hour after dinner and discussed things I couldn't have imagined a girl her age would know. The conversation was light hearted at first but soon took a downward turn. She appeared anxious and showed an odd concern for me.

She lowered her voice.

"You and your mother have to leave here," she explained. "You don't have much time. The man you think is my father..." She took a breath and continued. "Haven't you noticed that your guest list has been dwindling?" She held out a key and placed it in my clammy palm. "Look in the trunk of our horseless carriage if you don't believe me." Then a voice from the top of the staircase called out.

"Madeline!" Mr. Isaac said. I quickly placed the key in my pocket. "What did I tell you earlier?"

Her cheeks turned pallid. "Don't forget what I said," she whispered. As she stood, I noticed Mr. Isaac glaring at me; he didn't blink or move until she reached the top of the stairs.

I took Madeline's advice and decided to investigate the car. After waiting a short time, I walked outside and unlocked the wooden trunk that rested behind the spare tire.

It was dark inside, but the mystery of the missing houseguests had been solved. My heart plunged when I realized the trunk contained human extremities that appeared to have been cooked and partially eaten. Bloody arms and legs stained the interior, and the disembodied head of Mrs. Winter stared up at me. I recoiled and slammed the trunk.

I was afraid to go to bed that night as I had no way of locking my door. The best I could do was to prop a chair under the knob and hope it would hold. In the back of my mind, I knew it wouldn't, so each time I heard an outside noise, I jolted awake and abruptly sat up. But fatigue eventually won out, and sleep took over.

The next time I awoke, I was greeted by four blurry bodies that hovered over me and circled my bedside. I tried to move, but I was held down by what turned out to be a large harness. I noticed Madeline's tears glint in the moonlight as she stared at the floor, sobbing, while Mr. Isaac reached down and pulled something from my right arm. He asked how I was feeling as he eyed the sharp syringe.

I don't remember my response. I was queasy, and this was ninety-seven years ago, so I apologize for the lack of detail. What I do remember is their odd proposition. I was to come with them and never look back. They agreed to spare my mother if I conceited, but I was never to have any contact with her again, or she'd meet the same fate as the others. I already knew the answer, but foolishly asked what had become of them. "Dinner," was Mr. Isaac's response.

I am now exactly like them. A lifetime of experience hasn't changed my sixteen-year-old appearance, even as my mind has matured with one hundred and thirteen years of existence. I can't say it was all bad, but I sometimes wish they'd just gone through with their original plan to end my life and make me their next meal. But I did it to save my mother, and if Madeline hadn't convinced Mr. Isaac to spare us, we'd have been dead before morning.

I left with the Isaacs that night, and I kept my word never to see her again. It hurts to think of the hell the following years must've brought my mother, never knowing what had happened to me. I did return to the boarding house about six years later, but only to peek through the window to see if I could spot her. She wasn't there, and to this day, I don't know if she was dead or still alive, grieving me, and I hate them for it.

The Isaacs gave me immortality but made me an animal. I've killed many people in order to survive, but I can no longer do it. I will cease my actions no matter what my wife Madeline says, or does.

We aren't superfluous vampires or zombies— we're something much worse: a machine that survives only on human beings to keep ourselves young and viral and immortal. It's a terrible trade-off, and one that I've loathed my entire existence, but now I'm tired of hiding and have decided to expose my race as the monsters we are. There are many of us, thousands. We blend well with society, which makes us even more dangerous. As this entry goes public, let me just say, I'm sorry.

That Time of Year (Phil Thomas)

It was the first day of October in the small coastal town of Rockport, Massachusetts, and the locals were hard at work decorating their respective properties. Styrofoam tombstones, cheap cardboard skeletons, and harvest displays began popping up all over. At the same time, their mayor, Paul Taylor, was busy transforming the old vacant library into a haunted house for the "youngsters," as he called them.

As the whole town gradually turned black and orange, Detective John Sturgis was unable to share their enthusiasm. His nineteen-year-old daughter, Cynthia, disappeared in late August while returning home from a late-summer party with her boyfriend, Rocco.

Sturgis always despised him and immediately placed blame on the delinquent by throwing him to the top of his suspects' list. Deep down, however, he knew that Rocco wasn't responsible. This was a phenomenon that repeated itself every autumn in his town. Like clockwork, a resident would mysteriously go missing, never to be seen again. The first was Lucy Chambers back in 2005. It was the only significant black mark on the community and the one thing the detective had dreaded for the last fourteen years on the force. And now it had become personal.

Five agonizing weeks had passed and still no trace of Cynthia. If the past were any indication, those weeks would almost certainly turn into years, and his daughter would be just another victim on the growing list of statistics. As time slipped by, it became more challenging for Sturgis to function daily, so he took a leave of absence from the force to care for Cynthia's mother, who had suffered a full nervous breakdown after the first week.

On the second day of October, Sturgis was returning home from his morning coffee run and passed the spacious property of Mr. Pritchard, who had already unboxed all of his Halloween decorations and prepared his property two weeks prior for his favorite holiday. He had started with the interior before moving outside to his front lawn, where he established himself as the town's most elaborate decorator with scaled life-size replicas of zombies and ghosts and mummies and scarecrows, each with a disturbing depiction of torture or mutilation. Some of the creatures were carefully seated in vintage rocking chairs with others chained up or secured in padlocked stocks.

It was an annual occurrence that started shortly after Mr. Prichard had lost his wife to breast cancer. Still, every year since her departure, the townspeople could look forward to a new addition to his collection, which now equated to an appropriate fourteen pieces displayed behind his secured wrought iron fence—one decoration for each year that had passed.

The detective wasn't sure what had made him pull his car over to the side of the road that particular day to soak in the creepy atmosphere. It might have been fate or a low whisper in his subconscious, but as he left his car and walked to the front gate, he smiled for the first time since Cynthia's disappearance. The iron gate was unlocked, so he slipped in and circled around the property, admiring the goblin that sat along a tree branch, and the zombie that stood along the walkway, arms outstretched, seemingly searching for more brains.

An eerily familiar sight then caught his eye on the life-sized emerald witch shackled to Pritchard's tree. On the woman's left wrist was an elaborate tattoo of a black cat and the number 13 below it— the same tattoo his daughter had acquired earlier that spring.

As Sturgis entered the property and approached the witch, his skin pimpled at the realization that the arm wasn't made of plaster or fabric, but human skin. While sweat beaded on his forehead, he carefully pulled back the pointed nylon hat and lifted the rubber mask, laying his eyes upon the grey lifeless face of Cynthia. As he jumped back and assessed the other decorations on the lawn, he immediately concluded that these were the same folks who had delivered his mail, waited on him at the local supermarket, or fine-tuned his vehicle during annual inspections. They'd become a part of the twisted old man's permanent collection. He gingerly unmasked a tall ghost and scarecrow that were seated on a wooden bench, the familiar preserved faces of Bob and Donna Reilly slammed him like a steel girder as their unnatural grins and clouded sapphire eyes sliced back at him.

As he impulsively reached for his sidearm, he caught dead air, and a "click" sounded behind him. The officer spun and noticed Pritchard securing a padlock on his iron fence, a pistol tucked inside the waistband of his sweatpants. The old man grinned and slowly started towards him, cocking the hammer, and aiming it toward Sturgis. "My displays are meant to be enjoyed from street level," Prichard said in a glassy voice. "I can't imagine what you must think of me." Sturgis remained stock still, only raising his hands slightly. "I'm really not as bad as you might think," Prichard continued. "My displays bring joy to so many people each year. All of the faces you recognize here; their sacrifice hasn't been for nothing."

Sturgis broke himself from a numbing trance, glaring at the old man through kill-shot eyes, and whispered, "The witch here, that's my daughter, you son of a bitch." He sensed the rage coursing through his veins like poison. As a cop, he was sworn to uphold the law. But as a father, he wanted to kill this bastard.

Prichard lowered the gun at the realization. "You mean, you're Cynthia's father?" Sturgis nodded, his vision pinpricked, his fists clenched, and he knew that there would be no arrest made. There was no other scenario, but to see the old man dead. "Oh my," Prichard added, "she was a lovely woman, and I'm sorry for your loss. But that is why I wanted her for my display." Prichard walked to the tree where Cynthia's body was shackled. "Look at her, resting so majestic, immortalized, and frozen in time. I think she can bring more joy in her resting place than she would otherwise. Don't you agree?" Sturgis felt something snap inside. He rushed towards the old man, hoping to commandeer the firearm and discharge a strategically placed bullet between his eyes.

The whole scenario happened so quickly but played out almost in slow motion. When Prichard noticed Sturgis lunging towards him, he raised the pistol, but not before Sturgis grappled his arm, twisting it back and slamming his wrist against the tree. The firearm broke from the old man's grasp and landed on the lap of Cynthia. Her body hunched forward despite the shackles as the men struggled. Sturgis palmed Prichard's face and slammed the back of his head against the tree repeatedly.

As far as Sturgis was concerned, he wouldn't need a gun after all and was more than happy to kill the old man with his bare hands. After the fifth or sixth slam, Sturgis experienced an odd sensation on the nape of his neck, and then another on his top right shoulder

He craned his head and noticed a syringe dangling loosely from his flesh, the plunger depressed, its contents emptied. He made a desperate struggle to grasp the pointed instrument, but quickly comprehended he was unable to control his actions. His arms felt like fifty pounds of rubber, and his legs lost all sensation, failing him, collapsing underneath, and landing him on his back. He then stared straight up into the afternoon sun that beamed through the tree branches.

And the last thing that Sturgis saw was Prichard hovering over him before his world fell to dusk.

For the rest of the month, Mr. Pritchard wore a sinister smile because that particular autumn, he'd acquired not only one but two decorative trophies for his collection. He displayed them together.

124

Maveren Edge (Olivia Arieti)

The name was only mentioned a few times, but it had always caused a sense of awe in Gilbert before being wiped away like all childhood memories. Consequently, when Mr. Grant, the family administrator, communicated that he, now in his forties, had inherited Maveren Edge Estate no particular excitement occurred. The property belonged to his great-grandfather, Sir Anthony Maveren, and after the rather premature death of his descendants, Gilbert was the only heir left. An inveterate bachelor and with a good job in the city, he considered the legacy a fastidious issue well aware of the difficulty of selling such types of properties, too expensive to maintain and often marked as haunted. However, visiting the mansion and Mr. Grant who lived in the neighbouring town, couldn't be avoided.

The thick rain limited the visibility and the car had to make its way through a tortuous drive where fallen branches, overgrown shrubs and muddy pools had found their home.

Premonitory chills pervaded him on catching sight of the house that finally emerged in its adamant gravity through the ghastly mist.

The structure looked decayed, tarnished by time and lack of maintenance. The walls were tapestried by trails of ivy that had penetrated the many fissures, some shutters were falling apart, the lawn, an uncouth field fenced by skeletal hedgerows and the flowerbeds barren.

An inexplicable sensation of someone lurking in the vicinity seized him as soon as he got off the car; he shrugged and attributed it to the gloomy atmosphere of the site.

The new proprietor had to fatigue to open the door that stubbornly opposed to let him in.

Once inside, however, he marvelled before the sumptuousness of the halls, the frescos on the walls, the furniture that despite the layers of dust, maintained its imposing nobility. The knick-knacks were precious pieces of silver and porcelain, not to mention the many chandeliers, candelabras and the richness of the tapestry.

The four posted bed and its brocade drapes was so inviting that he had to give it a try. After lying down for a while, he unpacked, changed and descended the marble staircase.

Much to his surprise, the candles were lit and a pleasant fire was blazing in the fireplace. He looked around bewildered. Was his imagination playing tricks on him or was the place really haunted?

Touching the flame was the only way to find out.

He had just stretched out his hand when a raucous voice cried, "I wouldn't do that, Sir, you'll burn your finger."

He turned round instantly. Before him stood a middle aged lady, in a long grey robe that recalled a shroud. Her face was yellow, her eyes vitreous and Gilbert feared to be in front of a witch.

"I'm sorry I didn't come to greet you, but nobody informed me of your arrival, Mr. Maveren. I am Mrs. Delves, the housekeeper."

"Nobody has informed me of your existence," replied Gilbert disconcerted. "Are there other people in the house?"

"Miss Evelyn, Sir... She has the privilege of living here as she is a Maveren too."

Gilbert startled, "A Maveren too? She has never been mentioned by the administrator of the estate."

"She couldn't for her belonging to the family isn't known to anyone... Evelyn's mother was a maidservant here and when in her full bloom, our master with fake promises lured her into his room. The poor girl died of shame and of a broken heart shortly after her daughter's birth. On that same day, the rake wedded Lady Gertrude, the lascivious widow he was engaged with."

"A sad story, indeed," remarked Gilbert.

"Although Sir Maveren had never made his fatherhood official, he granted the child an honourable living. Since then, I raised Miss Evelyn as my own."

She added scornfully, "Quite a surprising resolution for a debauched fellow; this didn't spare him, however, from being stabbed to death, the knife stuck right in his heart."

"I didn't know Maveren Edge had been the scene of a murder," exclaimed Gilbert troubled.

"A most deserved demise, Sir, whether inflicted by a mortal hand or a spectral one," the housekeeper insinuated and left without giving him the chance to ask any questions.

127

The gentleman frowned; whatever happened in the past though, wasn't his business, but selling the property looked even more complicated. He had to ask the girl if she'd be willing to settle down elsewhere; of course, he would have to share the profits as well.

On entering the dining room, he noticed the table was set for two. A candelabra placed in the middle and a display of silver cutlery, porcelain dishes and crystal glasses on an embroidered tablecloth were ready for their evening diners.

The chance of having a taste of what must have been his predecessors' style of life pleased him and he couldn't help being fascinated by its great refinement.

His musing was interrupted by Evelyn's entrance. Never had he seen a more enticing girl. Although very thin, she had a sensual figure with long black hair falling upon her naked shoulders, her carnation as white as a porcelain doll. She needed no makeup for the lips were naturally crimson and the eyelashes long and thick.

"Glad to have some company this evening," she said, "it's quite lonely here."

Her smile was tight, but the eyes twinkled with vivacity, a morbid vivacity.

Although Evelyn didn't look old fashioned, she treasured the elegance and severity of a bygone past. She belonged to the mansion, like the marble statues in the halls that had heard all its arcane secrets and perhaps, witnessed the most forbidden deeds.

They had just finished dining when she gazed at him provocatively, almost defiantly.

"I've been told how my mother has been treated by the Maverens. I appreciated being granted a place to live, but am ashamed to be part of such a depraved family," she stated dryly.

An embarrassing silence followed.

"I don't know what happened actually, not even much about the Maverens, saw this place only once in a picture. The name is the only tie I have with them."

He felt as though attempting to excuse himself for bearing a name so rightfully despised by her distant relative.

The atmosphere grew tense. A malicious expression hardened the girl's face as if conjecturing something horrible. Her ominous desire made Gilbert shiver.

There was something unreal about her... She was as beautiful as an ethereal vision, but also as upsetting as a haunt. For sure, she was one of those deviant souls forever unfolding indefinite mirages that would fade and leave an unrequited wake behind.

Once in bed, Evelyn's image kept wavering before him; the lips slightly open waiting to be kissed while her body slowly freed itself from her satin dress and whatever was under it. Veiled by wantonness and cladded in mystery, she was mesmerising him and he couldn't do anything but surrender... An insalubrious itch seized him and kept him awake the whole night.

The cock's shrill cry at the crack of dawn was hailed with relief as the haunt, nightmare or delirium immediately vanished.

The following morning, Gilbert had breakfast alone. Mrs. Delves came down to inform him that Evelyn was not well and would have remained in her room the whole day.

He was about to take a drive around the property when Jason, the mansion's keeper, announced, "Mr. Grant's niece, Miss Amelia has arrived. Shall I show her in?"

Another unexpected presence, thought Gilbert, wondering who else would show up at Maveren Edge before he left.

Amelia was very pretty with a bright smile and sparkling eyes. Although in her twenties, she looked like a school girl, totally different from his previous girlfriends, all nervous, overexcited, only concerned with their career, body and money.

A research regarding the estates of the area was the reason of her visit.

"I hope you don't mind if I spend some hours in your library, Mr. Maveren, my uncle insisted I should ask your permission first."

"Not at all," he replied, "I'm eager to see the library too as I haven't been there yet."

The room was huge, two leather armchairs stood before a mahogany desk, a couch in front of the fireplace and the walls were covered by bookcases from the floor to the ceiling. His ancestor's portrait hung above the mantelpiece, the only free space left opposite the desk. Somehow, the

130

face appeared vicious with bulging eyes, drooping ruddy cheeks and the carnal lips curled in a vile sneer. Could he have been the perverse rake?

While his guest was searching through the books, Gilbert moved over to the window and right under the secular oak, he discerned Mrs. Delves's grim figure looking up. Was she spying on him?

"This book treasures all the information I need, Sir," said Amelia happily.

"Just Gilbert, I'm a down to earth city guy that somehow happened to turn into a country gentleman."

"That's not bad, the country's so serene and its beauty, unspoilt. Since my parents died, I've been staying with my uncle and I like it here."

"I reckon you're acquainted with Evelyn and Mrs. Delves. They both live in this house."

Amelia looked at him perplexed, "No, never met them... As a matter of fact, I didn't know anybody lived here except old Jason, the keeper."

Her reply surprised him and he tried to figure out why their presence went unnoticed.

"You can take the volume home and I'll be glad to read the work when you're through with it. I believe I, too, need to get acquainted with Maveren Edge's history..."

She was about to leave when he said, "I'm going to take a ride along the countryside, will you join me?"

He liked Amelia and wanted to spend more time with her.

After driving for about an hour, Gilbert stopped in front of a picturesque lake that was also part of the property.

"Good thing you came along, I didn't even know this lake existed."

"It's such an enchanting spot, I used to come here often, sometimes even took a dip. I loved watching the sun set behind those hill, the copper streaks turn purple and fade in twilight's dimness."

A deep sigh followed...

On distinguishing Gilbert's inquisitive look, she continued, "I stopped coming for I began seeing shadows among those willows and even heard strange moans... couldn't help being scared even if it was nothing but the work of my imagination."

Her face paled and she looked like a little girl afraid of the dark.

He took her hand and whispered, "That's normal, dear, when the sun goes down, these places gain a creepy aspect for whoever."

Somehow, he felt the need to protect her; her childish expression melted his heart.

Unexpectedly, the wind started wailing and the motionless surface swelled with ripples. The sky darkened and bleak shadows apparently, swayed in the distance.

The couple stood incredulous and doubtful of their own senses.

"Better get going," urged Gilbert and pulled his partner away.

'Too much eeriness around here,' he thought and was more than glad he didn't live in that grisly country corner.

They stopped at a coffee shop near Amelia's home. The place was small, the tables one next to the other, but the atmosphere was merry and the warm drink quickly dissolved all anxieties.

"It's nice talking to you, Amelia. By the way, there's also a volume two you should check."

"I've noticed that. If you don't mind, I'll drop in tomorrow afternoon. Oh, I forgot to tell you that my uncle's visiting a dear friend who had a bad accident and will be away for quite a while."

Gilbert wondered how long he would have to lodge at Maveren Edge.

"Hope I'll get to see you during my stay," he muttered, "never met a more charming girl than you."

Her cheeks flushed. Did she like him too?

"I wouldn't like to sound too straightforward, but could you also remain for dinner? I'm not used to staying alone in such a big house," he chuckled, "and quite afraid some ghosts may pop in."

"To tell the truth, the locals say the place is haunted, but that's quite common for isolated old mansions to be considered so. However, I'll be glad to dine with you."

She pressed her hand on his and her warmth pervaded him.

Mrs. Delves and Evelyn didn't come down the following day either. Gilbert didn't mind since their presence upset him. He kept thinking of Amelia and was anxious to see her again.

When the girl's car pulled up the drive, he was already on the doorstep.

The afternoon was spent in the library and afterwards, they took a walk around the house. Undoubtedly, nature had disowned the place and they had to do their best to imagine how lovely the garden, the bower and the lawn they must have been in their full splendour.

While heading towards the dining room, Gilbert distinguished a lugubrious figure slide against the wall and disappear into the adjacent room. He was about to follow it, but didn't want to keep Amelia waiting.

He wondered when the spectres had taken possession of the house if ever they did...

After dinner, the couple sipped their brandy before the fireplace. Gilbert couldn't deny he was falling for the sweet researcher; her gentle ways and innate enthusiasm filled his heart with joy.

They were sitting very close when he took her in arms and kissed her passionately unable to conceal his feelings any longer.

Amelia, too, had abandoned herself, tender and languid, anxious for his kisses and caresses.

He had always asked himself what would have followed if a sudden peal of thunder hadn't blasted their ears; the lights went out and the shutters banged open and shut. He leapt up and tried to close them, a pane broke and shards of glass hit him. When he turned round, he was dripping with blood.

Immediately, Amelia called Jason, bandages were provided and the wounds taken care of.

That was another sleepless night for the new owner. The cuts kept hurting and for no reason could he explain the improvised turbulence.

The thought of a wicked force domineering the place made him shudder.

Where were Evelyn and Mrs. Delves? Didn't they hear that damned peal as well?

As though reading his mind, the housekeeper knocked at his bedroom door.

"Miss Evelyn wants to see you," she said before vanishing in the corridor's darkness.

Gilbert was more vexed than agitated as he headed towards the girl's room.

"Come in," said Evelyn's hollow voice.

She smiled slyly, "I was waiting for you, dear."

"I want to know what's going on here," he thundered.

"No master of Maveren shall ever find peace in this house. I've been nourished with hatred against all the descendants when in my mother's womb, and her thirst for revenge is what makes my heart still palpitate. For this reason you have to die, bastard, the only way to wash away your bloody name's shame."

She took out a knife, "This is the knife my mother used to stab her dissolute seducer and now it will kill you too."

With all her might she thrust herself against him.

Rapidly, her potential victim's hand managed to grasp hers and the weapon plunged into her breast. A loud, unhuman cry resounded in the halls. As Evelyn fell, her body deflagrated; her only remains, a heap of sooty ashes.

At once, the cock's cry was heard from the fields.

Suddenly, everything was clear. "Glad you didn't make it," shouted Gilbert, "however, you did your best to revenge your mother, Evelyn. I'm sure you and your Mrs. Delves will rest in peace now."

That said, he shut the door behind him and went back to his room.

Early in the morning, Gilbert informed Jason of his immediate departure. The old man was upset and showed him the knife.

"I found it in Miss Evelyn's room. I saw the light on and heard unusual cries last night so I went to check that everything was alright."

He sighed, "She died so young too. Seems this house's lasses are all doomed to a tragic fate."

"What happened?" Gilbert asked eager to know the whole story.

"The weather was very bad when Evelyn and Mrs. Delves took that boat ride on the lake of your property, Sir, the vessel capsized and they were thrown into the water. Although small, it's very deep, a hellish abyss. Their bodies have never been found, but I'm sure their spirits have returned here."

Gilbert didn't care to investigate further; he had enough of the mansion, it ghosts and past dwellers.

There was still one thing he had to do before leaving, visit Amelia.

On seeing her, his happiness was such that he hugged her tight, "Listen, darling, I don't know how to say it because I've never said it before… I love you and want to marry you. As soon as I sell the property, I'll buy a big house where we can settle down with our family," he muttered, hopeful the mansion would sell well now that it was no longer haunted.

Amelia nodded slightly, her smile as radiant as ever.

Old Soul (Chris Rodriguez)

Sari set her antique doll, Christine, on the top of her overcrowded dresser. Usually, Christine sat on her bed against the pillows, but at night she slept better knowing the doll would not be damaged or knocked to the floor by accident. She had just taken her childhood doll to her lady's group to show her off. Cottonwood Cove Retirement Community had several groups and many activities to keep the residents busy. Some of the others brought things from their childhood as well, but Sari's doll was the oldest of any she had ever seen. When the ladies "oohed and ahhed" over her display of antique doll clothes that came with Christine, Sari felt special. She knew that Christine would be happy about the attention as well.

Some people thought dolls were only toys or objects to be displayed, but Christine demanded attention. When Sari's grandmother had given her the doll after her 8th birthday party, she warned Sari right off.

"Now Sarah Rose, I am passing Christine down to you, trusting you will keep her happy and in perfect condition. She will be your best friend or your worst enemy! It's up to you. Here are her clothes. Christine loves to look pretty, but you must be sure to keep them in good repair. Do you promise?"

"Yes, Grammy, I promise!" Sari was breathless with wonder and pride to think her grandmother trusted her with this precious possession, one Sari knew well as she had long admired the old doll on Grammy's bed – the one she had not been allowed to play with let alone touch.

Grammy held Christine one more time before handing it over to her granddaughter. Sari thought it odd that Grammy did not hold the doll close or hug it goodbye, but held it tightly in a fist a fair distance from her face and frowned. She even hesitated when she handed it over to Sari's outstretched arms.

Sari was almost an antique now herself, but never could pass down Christine since she didn't have a granddaughter which had been the custom for decades. It wasn't for lack of trying to find a new place for her. Sari had loaned Christine to many an 8-yr-old she felt could have been like a surrogate grandchild. But Christine had come back to her each time. Usually when the child fell ill or once when her best friend's granddaughter had died in an accidental fall while playing in her tree house with Christine. Sari felt especially bad about that since she had forgotten to tell the little girl that Christine was an indoor doll and hated high places. Sari did not share these stories with the ladies.

Now Sari was worried what would happen to Christine when she herself was gone. She wrote in her will that the valuable keepsake should be donated to a museum or a well-known doll collector but not for display. She knew Christine would not like being in one spot and one outfit for long. She would have to be kept locked in her special trunk with the funny writings on it. Her grandmother had called them Runes. The trunk would be stored in a temperature and moisture-controlled basement or attic with the key stored in a separate space in a locked safe. These instructions came with Christine along with her clothes and other accessories.

"There. We had a lovely outing, you and I. Now you should be happy for a while."

Christine's staring eyes cut to the side toward Sari's voice. Sari didn't notice as she made a mighty effort never to look at Christine unless she had to. It wasn't good to let Christine see her fear or nervousness. She continued to straighten her bed and gently moved the doll to sit against the pillows.

"Ow! You little devil!" Sari sucked at the blood on her finger. "Why did you do that?"

"Sari, what happened?" Her friend Karen had slipped into the apartment without her hearing. She wasn't supposed to come without informing Sari first, but she had a wilful mind of her own. "Here. Let me help you with that," she said as she handed Sari a tissue.

Karen grabbed a bandaid from Sari's medicine cabinet and applied it after Sari had washed and dried the tiny wound. "What did you cut it on?" Karen moved quickly back into the bedroom, her eyes stopping everywhere in curiosity and suspicion. In three years, she had never been allowed in her friend's bedroom.

"I don't know. Christine is very old. Maybe something flaking off or a metal pin. I'll look at her later."

Sari grabbed Karen's arm and tried to guide her from the bedroom. "C'mon. Let's go make a cup of tea."

140

But Karen dragged her arm back and marched to the bed to bend and peer closely at the doll sitting there in all her finery. "Uh, oh," she tsked. "I think she got a bit of blood on her little mouth. Let me wipe it real quick so it doesn't stain."

Sari lurched toward her friend and yanked her arm so hard, Karen yelped. "Sorry. I said I'd look at her later. I need a cup of tea now. In fact, let's go down to see Doris. She asked if we were doing anything this afternoon."

"But…!"

Sari yanked Karen's arm again and this time Karen followed along. When Sari glanced back at Christine, the blood was gone from the doll's rosebud mouth.

A few days later, Sari hobbled down to the dining room for lunch. She hadn't been able to get out to shop so had nothing left in her cupboards. She had no choice but to eat downstairs with the others. It was very warm, but Sari had donned long pants and a sweater.

"Sari, over here!" she heard Karen holler rudely from across the room.

Drat! Sari didn't really need her nosy friend asking questions, but knew she would. Her shoulders sagged in resignation as she shuffled to the table.

"Hello, Doris," she mumbled. How have you been?" She already knew how Karen was since the Nosy Nora called to grill her a couple of times a day.

"How are you?" Doris replied. "Karen has been keeping me informed. I hear you have been under the weather."

Sari fumed knowing full well Doris wasn't the only one Karen had been talking to about her business.

"Not sick!" Karen announced a little too loudly for Sari's comfort. "She says she took a fall. Personally, I think she needs to see a doctor. Been a lot of so-called accidents lately."

"That's not for you to worry about, Karen. I guess I'm old enough to know when I should go to a doctor," Sari snipped. "I'm a grown-assed woman and can take care of myself."

Doris looked away as Karen sniffed. "Someone got up on the wrong side today."

The three pals ate the rest of their meal in silence for fear of riling Sari again. Doris reached over and patted Sari's hand but intentionally avoided looking directly at the bruises crawling up Sari's arms when her sweater sleeves were pushed up. She wasn't about to address the issue and get a dressing down, too.

After lunch, they went upstairs to the activity room for a presentation by a local writer who was compiling stories about hauntings at Cottonwood Cove. Wanda, the activities director waved at them from her seat in the back row, but they moved closer so Doris could hear better. She was too vain to wear her hearing aids.

It was too hot outside and Sari thought the air-conditioned room would feel much better and give her an excuse to keep the sweater on. Normally, she enjoyed readings, but she fidgeted and was distracted by her dilemma. *Something needs to be done with Christine. And soon! I can't take much more of this.* Sari just didn't have the energy she had as a child to give the proper attention to the demanding doll. She knew what she needed to do to get some relief. She had done it many times before. Not wanting to think about it now, she finally focused her attention on her friends enjoying the stories of the place they lived.

That night she whispered to Christine who was tucked in beside her. The doll had refused to sit on the dresser for the past several nights. She had swept items off and broken Sari's mother's favorite Hummel, the one of the girl feeding the geese. It was worth a pretty penny as a collector's item, but meant the world to Sari as a sentimental piece. She had cried for hours after.

"Please, please don't make me do it again. I'll do anything you want," Sari bargained with Christine. The doll remained unmoving, its eyes closed as if asleep. Sari knew Christine was not asleep. Dolls never sleep.

When Sari trudged heavily down to the activity center to meet her friends the next day, her shoulders sagged in defeat. She absentmindedly touched the bandage on her neck and nodded in silent acknowledgement. She slid into a chair beside Doris who automatically reached to pat her friend's hand.

"Glad you made it! We were getting worried." Sari offered a half smile and squeezed Doris' hand back.

After the pleasant array of songs performed by a group of senior women called The Silver Belles featuring their good friend Loretta, Sari suggested they go outside to sit under the arbors now that the roses were in full bloom. She hoped it wouldn't be crowded with other residents who sometimes appeared for walks before dinner. No worries. The three friends sat in the shade near the sweet smell of the summer garden in front of them and the meadow grass in the long fields behind.

"What's bothering you these days?" Karen demanded of her friend. Doris looked away embarrassed that she could be so direct. "And what the heck is that on your neck? Is there something going on we need to know about?"

Sari kept her eyes firmly glued on the dancing colors in the garden. Bees buzzed sweetly in and out of fat blossoms, a flock of sparrows in a nearby bush, chattered busily. "Nothing! Why would you think something is wrong?"

"This stupid bandage on your neck for one thing," Karen said as she reached to touch it.

Sari pulled away and tried to cover the bandage with her hand, but Karen got to it first and managed to pull it partially off.

"What in the world?" Karen breathed. Doris even turned her head to gape at the wound on her friend's neck.

Sari hurried to recover the wound. "Something bit me. Haven't you ever had a bite? Probably a spider. This place hasn't been fumigated in forever." She had to cut her eyes away from her disbelieving

144

friends. Even Doris stared in horrified fascination, but still didn't utter a word.

"Sari. That is not a spider bite. It's... it's... Well, it looks like tiny little teeth marks!"

Sari laughed half-heartedly and replied, "That's ludicrous! What are you talking about? It's nothing," she claimed as she fumbled with the bandage. "I need to get back to my room. I'll see you both for dinner in the dining room this evening." She stalked off without looking back.

That evening Sari was the first to the table in the already packed dining area. She placed her room keys on the table beside her plate and drank half of her glass of water as her friends arrived. She smiled at each one, but looked nervous, fidgeting with the keys throughout the meal. Both friends noticed her actions and looked at each other with eyebrows raised in question. Normal conversation took over about what activities they should pursue over the next week, if they should take the transportation bus to shop for groceries, and the possibility of going on an afternoon field trip to a nature area. Oddly enough Sari opted for all of them.

After they had eaten, Sari jumped up and announced she needed to go for a walk to settle her stomach.

"Wait, we'll go with you," Doris said.

"That's okay, I need to think about some things." Sari stalked off as her friends looked at each other again, then shrugged.

Karen glanced down and noticed Sari had left her keys on the cleared table. She looked in the direction Sari had gone but didn't see her. She licked her lips and her eyes lit up. Karen picked up the keys and told Doris she was going to go meet Sari at her apartment to make sure she got her keys back. "We'll catch up with you for the movie later. Are you bringing the popcorn?"

Doris nodded and shuffled off toward the elevator. "See you soon, then."

At 7:00pm, Doris watched as Sari came toward her. She was alone and smiling brightly. Her old self again. Doris sighed in relief. She had been uncomfortable with whatever it was that had been happening with Sari and between her two best friends. As the lights lowered, she looked for Karen to join them. She was never late, especially for the movie. It was her pet peeve. She hated being late and hated when others were late and let them know in no uncertain terms.

Doris leaned over to whisper, "Where's Karen?"

Sari shrugged and laughed at the antics on the large screen TV.

Doris glanced behind her again, but couldn't shake off the feeling that something was wrong. "Did she bring you your keys? You left them on the table."

"Shhh! I'm watching the movie." Sari whispered. "Yes, she left them on my table in the hallway."

Doris nodded, then thought better of her instant relief. Karen would never have left the keys laying where anyone could get them and break into Sari's apartment. "But,…"

146

"Please, Doris! Let me watch the movie. I'm sure she just didn't feel like coming tonite."

Doris remained quiet, but nervous through the rest of the show. After the lights came on again, she said, "I'll call Karen and see if she's okay."

Sari shrugged. "Well, if you want to, but I hope she's not asleep. You know how she is when she's awakened."

Doris contemplated her past experience with this fact. "I'll wait until tomorrow morning then. I'll see you for breakfast?"

"No. No, I think I'll have a light breakfast on my deck tomorrow. I want to see the sunrise."

Sari waited for Doris to step into the elevator then headed for the stairs. At her apartment, she looked in both directions up and down the hall before unlocking her door and stepping in, the door closing hastily behind her. She rushed into her bedroom and was relieved to see Christine sitting in her spot on the bed, pillows propping her up. Her eyes were open and they clicked in Sari's direction.

"Did you get what you wanted?"

Christine's eyes closed briefly, then opened again. As her lips opened, a drop of blood spilled out.

"Oh, bother!" Sari moved toward the doll. "We better get you cleaned up and changed. I will need to change my bedding as well." After that chore was completed and it was full dark outside, Sari slipped out after once again checking the hall. Outside, she propped the door slightly open with a rock so it wouldn't lock behind her. She knew the security locks wouldn't be on yet as Kerry, the night

147

manager, was still doing rounds. She had to hurry though.

A quick check over the back fence behind the arbors showed what she already knew. Karen's red sweater draped over the dry meadow grass with matching red spots and blotches scattered around the area where her friend had tried to crawl away from her deadly stolen treasure. She was satisfied as she turned to head back. Sari saw Kerry through the window headed in the direction of her door so she hurried toward it.

"Oh, you're lucky. I was just about to lock all these doors for the night," Kerry told her gruffly. "You're cutting those walks pretty close!"

"Yes, it's very dark at this time of night. I couldn't see a thing." Sari squeezed by without an apology and with a spring in her step, returned to her room. She hadn't felt this good in months.

148

Eleanora (Paul Edwards)

Lauren felt two things as she watched the late evening news – empathy for the mother pleading for the safe return of her child, and a sudden jolt of fear that Eleanora might visit tonight.

The chime of the clock in the hall interrupted her thoughts. She left her chair and stared out the window at the shivering fences and pitch-black sky. Like a drumbeat, the rain rapped steadily against the window.

"Please, whoever has her… bring her back…"

The mother's eyes were red-rimmed and smudged with mascara, her voice choked, desperate, and pained. There was a deepthroated growl of thunder, and the picture on the television skipped a couple of times before righting itself.

"We just need to know that our little girl is okay…"

It's been fourteen days now, since Eleanora was here last, but Lauren couldn't remember a single thing about it. Perhaps that was a blessing, judging by the newspaper clippings she'd found in a shoebox under the bed. But she didn't want to think about that now. Didn't want to think about Eleanora, either – Eleanora was so powerful, so dominant…

Another muttering of thunder. Rain sloshed and gurgled through broken guttering. The mother was escorted out of the press conference to a flurry of camera-flashes. Lauren felt for her, particularly now

149

she was a mother herself. "It must be awful to lose a child and not know where it's gone," she sighed.

It reminded her that it was time to check in on her own little one. She switched off the television, the chatter of the rain intensifying around her.

Just as she was about to snatch shut the curtains, a flash of lightning illuminated the small mounds of earth out in the garden.

***

"Sweet dreams, angel."

Lauren leant over the cot and smoothed down tufts of the child's spiky blond hair. The child whimpered and cooed softly in her sleep. How could anyone want to harm something so innocent, so beautiful, Lauren thought? It made her afraid of the dark, of the news on TV, of the clock ticking downstairs in the hall. The child rolled over but remained asleep, her face a pale oval in the shadows playing across the room.

"Love you," Lauren whispered, planting a kiss on the child's forehead. "I could never do anything to hurt you. You know that."

Lightning sketched shadows across the nursery. The rain hissed a name against the window, over and over: Eleanora, Eleanora, Eleanora...

***

Lauren closed the nursery door and drifted off into the bathroom. It was pitch black there.

Suddenly, a flash.

Her face filled the mirror – skin as bloodless as parchment, black-smudged eyes, snakes of straggly dark hair splashed over bony, angular shoulders.

Then darkness again.

150

Downstairs, the clock ticked like a heart.

She opened her mouth to speak, but what spilled out wasn't her voice.

"Hello Lauren. You've got something for me, haven't you, dearie?"

Lauren couldn't reply – she was curling up inside herself, like a small animal going into hibernation. Her hand balled up. Then it punched glass, cracking the mirror into a web. Trembling fingers prised out a jagged sliver of glass, spattered with gorgeously dark droplets of blood.

Thunder shook the house. Lightning washed new shadows across the walls.

Eleanora shrank away from the mirror, cackling maniacally to herself as she edged along the landing toward the nursery.

Curve of the Dagger's Blade
(Rickey Rivers Jr.)

I've been walking for some time in the spacious desert of northern Africa. I'm lost. The heat of the great sun makes my vision blurry, my mind hazy. I haven't seen a person in days. My water supply replenishes, yet my tongue is grainy and bitter. Still, I walk on, one foot in front of the other, pushing down on the desert sand which seems unmoving if only grain by damnedest grain.

I wasn't always here, or listless. I was once deep in the tomb recently unearthed in my travels. My colleagues and I were dead set on discovering the secrets of the tomb. This tomb, built stone by stone, stood great and grand near Old Dongola. We were directed to its location by the natives. Our translator, Maya, told us the tale of the old, deserted town, how its people had suffered, but this tale was of no use in reference to the tomb itself.

The tomb, circular in nature, was embedded within the sand of the desert. We had to dig for days to find an entrance. This entrance was merely stone which needed to be removed, a primitive and practical way to avoid intrusion. Nevertheless, my team and I found a way around the stone. Pushing sand away from the edges, we were able to make an opening wide enough for each of us to shimmy into the tomb. Once inside we were able to survey our surroundings. The tomb stood rank with foul odor.

Noses were covered, flashlights were out, and we began to document.

***

I say, the tomb was indeed elaborate, stone upon stone with twisting hallways. I remember being reminded of the catacombs in Paris. Luckily, we were wise enough to leave a trail of rags leading from the entrance to our location. When need be, we'd change the direction of the rags to reflect our current location. Our plan was to document one section at a time. It would take months to document it all. But we were only exploring for a week, the initial digging took longer than expected.

The first night we slept in the tomb. It was quiet and cold. The distinct feeling of loneliness enraptured us. We kept ourselves busy with card games. All in all it went well. Night two was the real bother.

On night two we heard sounds. These sounds were like whispers. Maya couldn't deceiver the language. Still, we slept in the tomb once more. Though sleeping was less than pleasant.

On the third day a discovery was made, a stone coffin deep in the middle of the tomb. We were intrigued. A plan was decided. All of us wanted documentation of the contents of the coffin, but it was nearly impossible to shift the weight of the great stone tablet weighing down the coffin's interior. We needed more men inside the tomb to help us remove the tablet. Of course the men of the continent could help, but many were afraid to follow us into the desert and furthermore into the tomb. One man had joined initially for the digging,

153

but even he refused to walk foot behind us into the opening.

Still, our minds were intrigued with the coffin. On the third night all of us slept around it. Before sleeping we were trying to put together a plan that made sense, so that the contents of the coffin could at last be documented.

On this third night I had a terrible dream. I was sitting and staring at the unopened coffin, the great stone tablet still in its place. Then, there came a sudden movement. And the tablet began to slide from its placement. I distinctly remember the horrible sound of stone dragging against stone. Curiosity took over. I stood, and peered into the half opened coffin. There was nothing inside but a corpse. Upon further inspection the corpse seemed to be clutching something. I reached into the coffin and grabbed what the figure was holding.

I saw then in my hands a great curved dagger. It's making no doubt by keen hands, a sleek and supple design. I took note of the corpse in the coffin, its sunken scowl of anguish, the twisted bones, the shape of torment; I didn't notice or seem to care, but I had broken the finger bones of the corpse when I grabbed the dagger. I apologized, and Maya stood up. The rest of my colleagues followed, and they then went peeking into the coffin. All of them surrounding it like shadows in the night. In a flash I was awaken, and in the same position of the coffin I saw red. Several of my colleagues had been displayed on the walls of the coffin room, and they were split open.

***

154

I followed the rags away from the coffin room and headed toward the exit. I'm ashamed to say I left my colleagues behind. Shimmying through the opening I thought I saw a native in the night, but the night only revealed itself the beautiful North African desert. The moon shone over the desert sand, and I found myself walking in the blue until the blue became orange then red.

The sun replaced the moon, and still I'm walking past where the great tomb was. And I know that I won't see my colleagues anymore, or the natives anymore, much less animal or recognizable plant. All that remains in sight is the dagger, the wonderful curve of its blade.

As I peer into the curve I sometimes imagine myself pushing the blade into the center section of my core. The flesh made an opening, and then came the sea like the open blackness of the tomb. I see the vision of sliding stone away from me. I remove my sight from the blade and continue walking.

I think back to the night of the dream, the blade in one hand, looking down seeing the sight of the other hand clutching brown and lovely hair, the scalp dangling, Maya dripping from the dagger's wrath. I think back to that dream, and I keep the dagger close.

Bringer of the Globe (Rickey Rivers Jr.)

The fireplace warms the cabin. I sleep near the cracking fire. In the orange light I sit in silence, my shadow bouncing on the wall. The cold wind blows past the windows. The snow is visible from every angle. The mountain range looms. I dare not trek to reach them. I stay near the fire. This place is not my home.

I discovered the cabin once waking up in the snow. It took a while to reach this place. Beyond the mountains it's the only recognizable object (for lack of a better word) to be seen in this weather, and this weather has been nothing but snow for days. Everyday I run low on food and firewood, but every morning, after waking, both provisions have been replenished. Again, this is not my home.

I do remember my home, my neighborhood. I'm a schoolteacher. I live on Basin Street in Daphne Alabama. I teach history at Great Oaks High, but none of this means anything. The only thing that matters is hell, this one.

I've tried several times to walk around the cabin. At daybreak I take small treks and watch the mountain range. I've taken a chair and used it to climb atop the cabin. There's nothing in my line of sight, nothing but white. The cold chills. At night it aches my bones, a walk to the restroom is a slow torture, any distance is, away from the fire.

Fire is sustenance, above food even, as the food is the same. Everyday the same meal or meals, broth, bread and meat. I don't know the source of either item. I do know that I've been provided with table salt, pepper and paper towels. I suppose that's all a man needs to survive. After all, I have the fire.

Sleep is peace. I long for it as a dove longs for love. I equate this to Aphrodite, the Greek goddess. Beyond history, mythology is a hobby. There's so much time now to read, so much time do anything, but books were not provided. There's so much time that I have to carve out bits of the past in order to remember them. Lest I be forgotten as a teacher lost in time to some great tragedy. My students will, I hope, remember me.

As for my wrongdoing or crime, I assure you I'm innocent. Yet I suffer in this hell, as a sinner who's unlike a simple man such as myself. No, perhaps I'm not so innocent. Perhaps I'm like you, a sinner by ignorance. I'll relay what I know of my past before the moments of waking on the snow, before meeting my new home, before the long nights in the cabin, with the sounds outside, the shuffling, the muttering, some sort of ancient babble from beneath the snow, it almost a living thing. The snow itself a blanket, possibly covering some grand scheme, a backstage curtain to hide an ultimate truth. But what is truth, and what could the snow possible hide?

***

The day before the snow I was off work and leaving the classroom. Again, Great Oaks High, I taught history. My name is Simon Dempsey. After

157

finishing papers I left the school and went to purchase a gift for my son, Eric. I love that little guy.

Eric was the product of my previous marriage to his mom, Pauline. Pauline and I separated after a misunderstanding. The misunderstanding was something that was built up over time. It's never just one thing that causes a separation. It hadn't been working for us for a while. It was finally time for one party to get it over and done with, and once that party decided they were finished, that's when the whole situation was sped up and the papers were signed.

Back to my son, Eric, a young boy who only wanted love and toys. He liked baseball, hockey and something sweet after a cheese pizza. His mother couldn't recognize the importance of staying together, keeping a family sane and safe, with all of us in the same household. No, she needed her time alone, her peace, she valued her sanity over marriage.

Anyway, after school a gift for Eric was the goal, so I went to the mall to shop for him. The toy store didn't have what I wanted. This gift was to be an action figure, one that released to coincide with a superhero film that was soon to be released. I didn't understand why Eric wanted the action figure before seeing the film. Nevertheless, I'm Dad and Dad gets what his kid wants, because Eric is my only son and I love him so much.

After leaving both toy stores in the mall I almost left until I was flagged down from outside a video game store by a man selling cheap jewelry in the middle of the mall.

"Need jewels for your lady?"

"No thanks," I told him, waving, almost shewing this man as I would a fly.

"How about a snow globe?"

***

Isn't it interesting how someone can not know you at all, yet still have exactly what you need and want at the moment you need and want it? Of course, I was there for Eric but I, being selfish, thought of myself. And why shouldn't I think of myself from time to time? Where's the love for the father in this day and age?

When I was a boy I loved a good snow globe. I use to get one from every state my parents and I visited. My father always let me get one, just one from every state, no more, no less. I loved my father and both my parents. They didn't let me have anything less. They understood the importance of a two parent household. This is what I wanted for Eric.

Now, a snow globe is simple by design, but that's the beauty of it. I have one with all sorts of insides. One snow globe has a snowman outside of a cottage. One has a snow covered beach with beach chairs, beach balls and a sand castle. One is full of children at a playground, when you shake the globe you can make the little girl on the swing set spin. It's lovely, simple. The simple things in life, they truly do matter.

As for the man waving me down from the mall kiosk. He did sell me a snow globe. He was a slick

159

talker. Yes, but I didn't feel swindled, not at the time. The snow globe, given to me, specifically to me, was one with a mountain range inside. I know where your line of thinking would lead you next, but I never saw the truth, not at the time. I never saw the cabin, until I was there.

***

I realize description of the man is needed. I have two descriptions. The first is of the outer man, the man seen as we see each other everyday. This man was like any other, if a bit scraggly, unshaven, with tired eyes and dry skin. He wore a winter coat and a beanie. His hair was brown and mostly hidden, only a few strands could be seen behind his ears. He smelled like cheap cologne, possibly purchased from inside the mall that very day.

The second description is of the inner man, the man not to be seen. This man had scaled skin, his forehead slumped, his nose was slim but flared. This man had small but bulbous eyes, they seemed to be on the verge of popping like boils filled with pus. This man was a shape, akin to another man inside of a smaller man. Staring at this inner man is the reason for my purchase. Sure, I wanted the snow globe, but common sense told me that I was shopping for Eric. However, in speaking with the outer man the inner man's influence seemed to speak louder.

This inner man or hidden man was the bringer of the globe, and I, of course, the buyer. I realized over time that the outer man had no say so in the matter. I wasn't speaking to him, neither was I purchasing anything from this shell of an almost person. I was merely given something from one hand to another, as if the skeletal frame of a person could work independently of that person. That's my predicament, buying something foreign from a person who wasn't a person, yet I won't be believed. The real story in the papers would be a fabrication.

"Local schoolteacher kills ex-wife and son."

Nothing of the snow globe would matter, only would the words. The man, inner or otherwise, is seemingly unimportant. Like the globe of the snow globe is less important than the inside of the globe. That's what people want to see. That's what they like; the scenery, the variety of locals, the projection of our world miniaturized, encased in glass.

It's possible to see your reflection in any snow globe. I remember not seeing much beyond the mountain range once staring at the globe outside the mall. My transport wasn't immediate, but I could feel the chill of the snow before I arrived at the cabin. In reality it was merely spring.

I wonder if the man is still at that mall kiosk in Daphne Alabama. I wonder if he's still selling globes or other items of misfortune. I wonder if he's laughing at me, and sometimes I wonder if that snow globe is still the outside world. Is it possible for you to find it? Is it possible for you to help?

I'm writing this down. If you find a snow globe in Daphne Alabama, one with a snowy mountain range, look beyond the mountains and find the log cabin. I'll be there. Break the snow globe, read the small, printed papers under a telescope, and find the man inside.

161

I'm here, but this is the only thing I can do at the moment. I know beyond the mountain range is glass, and I know it must be broken from the outside. If you break the globe and it kills me, let Eric Dempsey know that Daddy loves him and always will.

Kitty and Mr. Mouse (Rickey Rivers Jr.)

Ronnie lay curled on the couch. She flipped pages of an old magazine, catching words between the flips, taking note of the pictures, models with sequin. She was a model. She could have gone further if she had the mind, but she didn't have interest after some time. The runways were different, at least they became so.

"What a boring day," said Ronnie, perched on polyester.

Mavis kept his head down, the novel had his attention. He'd often take time to read away from Ronnie, but today Ronnie wanted to hang around. In fact, today she refused to leave home, canceling prior plans for brunch.

"How much longer?" she said, digging fingers into the couch to make noise.

Mavis kept his focus on the novel. "Why don't you go into the other room, watch television, maybe go to the store? I'm sure we need something, we always do."

Ronnie bit her bottom lip. "I don't want to go to the store, not by myself."

He flipped a page and read on.

"What book even is that?"

"It's called 'Quiet Moments and how I wish I had them.'"

"What's it about?"

He chuckled.

"What?"

"It's about a man on a journey. He gets lost and has to find his way home. He's searching for something someone stole from him. It's interesting."

"Sounds boring"

"He meets a woman in danger and wants to help her. They seem to have chemistry."

"Boring"

Mavis went on reading. Ronnie waited for him to speak so she could say it was boring all over again. But Mavis was ignoring her now. The only sound near was the clock overhead and the cars passing beyond the walls of home. She turned her head to watch them. Everyone else had places to go, things to do, people to see. She only had her husband and model friends. Which normally was enough, but it was supposed to be better than this. That's what she thought anyway. Life wasn't meant to be dull.

"How many pages in all?" she said.

He turned the book over and glanced at the last page, giving careful attention not to see the last words, "three hundred eighty one."

"Uneven dreck," she said.

She had a thing about uneven amounts of anything. She added more or took away something from something else just to make the numbers make sense in her head. On past runways she used to count her steps. She was always like this. Mavis knew, he didn't care. She was his wife, and at times a thing to deal with.

Ronnie made a noise like coughing up a hairball. He grimaced.

"Actually it's not too bad," he said. "I've read much longer."

Something about her amused him. He wasn't sure what it was. At times she was childlike in nature. At other times she reminded him of a cat, semi-independent, yet wanting attention all the same. She was a pet, but also his wife. He read on.

Ronnie made another sound, stretching, arching her back toward the ceiling and the floor. She gave him a soft glance, an offer. She then made noise like a yawn but drawn out.

Mavis read on, yawning himself.

"Sleepy?" she said.

"No."

Once before in the library Ronnie had made similar noises while Mavis browsed the aisles. These noises where accompanied by groping and whispers.

"You're going to get us banned," Mavis had said.

But Ronnie didn't mind. A trip to the restroom sorted her. A quickie in a clean stall was better than nothing. Ronnie had said so herself.

At another time on a flight back from Paris, again Ronnie was groping and making noises, and again the cramped restroom satisfied her. However, the satisfaction was one sided. Mavis had felt this way for a while. A relationship was one thing, fun and games, but marriage was a different reality.

Presently, Ronnie butterflied herself on the couch with her legs open and her head back, looking at the upside down cars pass on the road behind her. She made more noise, her tongue reaching for the sky, wagging, like the air was full of flavor.

"We're not animals," he reminded.

"I am."

For a moment there was silence, and to stop that Ronnie made ticking sounds to match the ticks of the wall clock. From there Mavis left the novel behind. He let his mind travel a bit, and thoughts came to him. Ronnie succeeded.

His mind took him to a different place, a different time, a grassy field, a cozy spot under a flowing tree. Flowers bloomed around the base, the sun shone overhead, and the weather was nice. He smiled with his eyes on the words in the book. He painted a peaceful image.

Soon Ronnie went interrupting again. She was making sounds and rolling on the floor.

He sat the book down and watched her. Ronnie clawed at the carpet and arched her back again.

"Please," she said. "Please.'"

He sat there staring. This woman was not his wife. She was different, strange to him, annoying. He adjusted his glasses and thought to himself. He wondered if her mind had regressed, if marriage had the ability to change a woman. He wondered if he should speak to a doctor. Then he thought again, the reality of doing so would be embarrassing.

He shook his head and stood up. "Does kitty want to play?"

'Kitty' was the pet name given. 'Kitty' was what she was, kitty and kiddy. Mavis had told her this, with D's replacing T's, and she ignored him. It was an age thing. They had years between them.

Kitty (Ronnie) rolled onto her back with her 'paws' in the air. Mavis knelt down and put a hand on her stomach. Soon his fingers went elsewhere. Up the chest and down again like brushing a canvas, he went on like this, teasing.

"Is Mr. Mouse a happy mouse?" said Kitty.

And Mavis went on with the game, smiling.

"Are you happy, Mr. Mouse?"

He was. He was happy and not there anymore. In his head he was someplace pleasant. Mavis knelt down further and his fingers went the opposite direction. He was right next to her ear. Ronnie was breathing heavy, gazing at the ceiling.

In his mind he was barefoot in a field. The sun warmed his toes. He sat down under a tree and read. Birds were chirping. Cars were passing.

In reality Mavis was next to Ronnie's ear and whispering. They wrestled from the living room to the bedroom. Mavis was there, but not there. Ronnie was happy again.

2.

He didn't hide anything. He went to the store covered in blood. He went through the sliding glass doors and grabbed a shopping cart. He grabbed milk, eggs, bread and cinnamon. People were whispering and someone might have screamed, but it didn't matter because Mavis couldn't hear anything, not in reality.

Police arrived shortly after he reached the parking lot. He was soon arrested. He didn't resist. He only asked to take the groceries home. The police allowed him to show them where he lived. That's when they saw what he did.

Ronnie Roe-Carson was displayed on the news for a full month. Models from all over attended her funeral. She was said to be a kind-hearted woman with dreams of living a peaceful life. People spoke of her philanthropy and how she could mimic animals. Her cat sounds were a dinner discussion topic. A YouTube video was spread of her appearing on a nightly talk show. There she interviewed a veterinarian and helped him feed a baby chimp.

Mavis was still in his head reading under a tree while birds chirped and butterflies floated. He was said to have good behavior. For morale a small Mesquite tree was planted in the prison courtyard. There he would read.

On different occasions he requested a book at the prison library. This was the same book he'd read at home. He never got a chance to finish it. Ronnie Roe-Carson had fans in prison too. She was a model, and she was his wife.

Dead In The Water (Liam A. Spinage)

I ain't gonna start this story telling you all about where my momma was born, or how she chose to live her life. I reckon that ain't exactly my story to tell on account of it being her story, and I'd only tell it poorly anyway and my brother would read it and disagree with every word. We're like chalk and cheese, me and him, on account of we both started out the same - that covers the 'ch' at the beginning of the words - and then diverge as wildly as two people possibly can who grew up under the same corrugated iron roof in the same backwater hicksville in the same Louisiana swamp.

I'm telling this for the both of us, writing it too so there's a record of what went down. And I'm telling it too for me, selfishly, because garbling this out is way cheaper than the local rye and a lot less trouble to make than moonshine. What happened that night haunts me still. As well it should, you might say. Well, you might, assuming I ever get to the matter of it, so I reckon I'll do that now and save you the whole David Copperfield crap, as Holden Caulfield was right about that. It'll only be relevant when I'm talking to my brother or, later, to our momma, and I reckon you'll get the handle of our sad little lives from those sad little snippets of conversation.

So, I'll start where this story really starts, with the news that momma had finally given in to the big

C, which had bothered her and worried us for so many of her later years. I like to think that when she finally went, she did it with the quiet dignity she'd kept up her whole darned life, but my brother Sammy says she went kicking and screaming, like she was being dragged somewhere she didn't want to go, and he should know because he was there and I wasn't and that was the main sticking point between us both from that day till now, on account of I was half a world away and he had to do all the legal work and all the paperwork and all the legwork until he was sick of it. I know that couldn't have been easy, but I didn't have much of a choice, the prison didn't sign my temporary release papers for an age and even then only let me have one day out to bury her and one day either side for travel and promised there would be hell to pay if I didn't make it back. To prove it, I'd been fitted with a new top-of-the-range ankle tag and the set of clothes I'd come in with - now two sizes too big - and stood outside the prison gates, blinking into the harsh heat of the southern sun and wondering whether Sammy had got my message about when to pick me up.

He hadn't.

I didn't hang around for him, that would have been dumb as dirt, so I started out down the road, just one more loner kicking up dust and hitching for a ride. Of course, no darn fool was about to pick up a hiker on the road that led to the prison, so I ended up walking in the blistering sun all the way to the nearest town. Drenched in sweat, I called Sammy - no answer - and then called a cab. It took some persuading to get him to drive me all the way, but I begged at him until I guess the goodness of his big ol' heart at last heard my plea and he ushered me into the back where I sat quietly the whole way, drifting in and out of sleep until he sounded the horn loud enough to wake up the dead and told me we were there and how much my brother owed him. Sammy came slouching out of the ol' house and calmly counted out a big roll of bills without so much as giving me a glance. Finally, when the driver had accepted a jug of water and been sent back on his way, we stood facing each other on the porch, my hands in my pockets, his by his side.

"Welcome home, Marti. Better come in and clean up. We gotta be at the funeral place in an hour." He turned and wandered back into the shack, then turned back again as if in afterthought.

"It's good to see you, bro."

***

"We've had to add mud to the cemetery, build a little levee, keep it above the tide line. It doesn't always keep the river at bay though." The old guy paused for effect, smug at his little maritime joke. Neither of us were amused. I guess coroners, gravediggers and the like mostly had a morbid sense of humour, but I also reckon they're used to keeping that in check around clients. This dude didn't even try.

He looked down at a map he'd laid out on the table for us in advance of the meeting my brother had asked for. One glimpse over at his assistant, though, told me she'd either been the one that had got the map ready, perhaps at his command, or had been the one who suggested it. Even so, despite the

171

air of goth kid indifference she clearly tried hard to muster with her all-back ensemble, there was more feeling in those eyes than the watery grey of the coroners. I'd seen more warmth in the eyes of my dead momma, Maisie May.

"We marked out all the gravestones with bamboo crosses before we undertook the clearance to keep it above water." He held up a clipboard and ran down it with a pen whilst humming some ditty I didn't know. In other circumstances, it might have been heartwarming. I doubted anything could warm his heart, though, and standing alone in this cold stone room did nothing but echo the eerie loneliness of that tune around the office. "Shouldn't be too hard to cross reference with the…bear with me…" His pen ran back up the page and stopped halfway. "Ah, here we are, plot 282A, Maisie May Wittie." He put a big red X on the map with a sharpie he kept in his top pocket, then rolled it up and handed it to Sammy. "Everything else is taken care of. Joshua is waiting at the jetty with the coffin and your ma."

That was that. No big ceremony, no wailing and gnashing of teeth. Sammy hadn't even organised a wake for later, on account of everyone else she knew had already said goodbye to her. We were taking her to where she'd spend eternity, on a little hill above a sunken graveyard just outta town and down the river. Right next to poppa. I didn't like that, but it was apparently too late to say or do anything about it, on account of how Sammy had already paid for the plot and decided that's where she should be. I thought he was wrong, but on this occasion, I knew something he didn't, and I wasn't about to tell him if I could avoid it. Even brothers have secrets. Blood might be thicker than water, but it can go bad just as fast and when it does, it's just as hard to clean up.

***

You ever seen a mangrove swamp? No? The dead trees already look like they've been fetched in from the film set of some horror movie. When you add to that the low mist of the evening and the occasional bright glimpse of the moon behind ever-growing clouds of black and grey, the effect was complete even before we got to the graveyard. On the raft over, Sammy had tried to impress on me that the water wasn't just due to the rising tide. Sometimes the river delta flooded. There was also something called groundwater extraction and something else called subsidence. I let most of this pass me by with a series of quiet nods. I didn't have pressure of speech like my kid brother, didn't feel the need to impress my knowledge on the world. I was largely content to let things happen to me and then weather the storm. Life by experience, not by book learning. You might call that the hard way, but then you're probably not as fucked up as I am so that's fine. When my folks were young, so they used to say, most of this area was still farmland. My parents were of the generation that stopped being farmers and started being fisherfolk instead. Adapting with the times just as I was trying to. The river delta, the sea, the periodic floods, they'd changed everything about how we all lived, and now apparently how people died as well. When I left, I didn't know if I'd ever be back. Apparently, fate had given me one last chance to say goodbye, but there had been nothing in the town I remembered well enough to say goodbye to, just a jumbled-up mishmash of memories, most of them bad.

I'd hoped that the most challenging thing we'd face on the way to the cemetery island would be the mosquitoes. From dusk till dawn, most people here slept inside mosquito netting, there were so many of them. There were too many mosquitoes, way too many flies, and a bad smell coming from the water.

I ran my hand idly through the water over the side of the raft. Apparently, even that was a dumb idea.

"Hands outta the water, Marti."

"Huh? Why?"

"Ticks. Bilharzia. Toxic grasses. Plus, the sludge, see, over there, that's new. Bubbles up every time they open the sluice on the dam further up. Whatever they put in the water up there ends up down here. Chemicals. Fertilisers. That kind of stuff."

"And Old Bessie!" The raft ferryman spoke up.

"Old Bessie's still here?" My brother looked surprised. I smirked. I figured he knew everything' so it was a pleasure when he got caught out.

"Who's Old Bessie?" I'd already removed my hand from the murk and was wiping it on my trousers. I'd have to throw them away after this anyway, they already stank of swamp water.

174

"You don't remember Old Bessie?" Sammy looked over. "Momma and poppa talked of her often enough.

"I remember 'em threatening to take me to her if I played up." I'd been a good kid, mostly, quiet and subdued because I didn't want to be the one that got the hiding from poppa. When I got into trouble, I made sure they didn't know and if anyone else told them, they'd never let on or told on me. But then, I'd always been the favourite. Up until that last day.

"Old Bessie is an alligator. Biggest alligator in these parts. She's still here, must be getting old by now. What they call long-in-the-tooth. Still made good work of Remi's leg last year when he got drunk on his fishing boat, though."

I was never so glad my hand was no longer in that water. Just when I thought I couldn't get more scared, I saw something move just beneath the surface. I recoiled slightly, huddling closer to the centre of the raft, which caused it to rock silently. Two rounds of tuts, from my brother and the ferryman both.

"Did you see that? Was that her?"

"Nah." The ferryman was evidently done with his chewing baccy and spat a great wad of it over the side. "Probably just a snake."

"You might have added snakes to the list of dangers."

"Everyone knows about snakes."

"Maybe I forgot."

Yeah, you'll have noticed that line about poppa. So, I'd better go into that more, I guess, since it'll be good to know given what's about to happen. Poppa could be a mean son of a bitch. Momma always said it was the whisky made him that way, that when they met, he'd been sweeter than peach cobbler. Now, I don't reckon that's the whole truth, but it sure felt like it as a kid. We'd come to recognise that particular look in his bloodshot eyes when he was about to blow his top. When he leaned down to shout at us, we could smell the sour reek of his whisky breath. But by then it was too late, the demon already had its hold and all we could do - momma included - was to ride it out until there wasn't any whisky left or until he was sleeping it off. Then we'd huddle together, and momma would patch us up as best she could through eyes full of fear and tears. Lord alone knows how we got through those days but somehow, we did.

My father worked odd jobs, mostly, when he worked at all. He hadn't the patience for fishing or farming but when he was sober, he was pretty good at fixing stuff up. When we were growing up, he'd often take the raft across the river to the rest of the town, because even then the river had swollen past the height of the bridge. When he came back in the evening, we'd sometimes wait for him by the jetty. If he'd gotten a couple of jobs and was in a good mood, he'd often have little gifts for us, treasures he'd made from trash or found in the river - bottle tops that had got stuck in a stone somehow and polished by the smooth flowing water or model cars that he'd wrenched together from twisted bits of metal. They were never much to look at, but we loved them.

Then things started to turn sour. Reckon as how I can't remember exactly when, on account of that's the bit of my life I wanted more than anything to block out, pretend it never happened. Every month or so, the river would be riding so high and so fast that the raft wouldn't run. If that happened in the morning, poppa would just mope around the house, lashing out at us for being in his way. If it happened in the evening, he'd be stuck over the other side of town, where the bar was. During one particular rainy season, we didn't see him for weeks and ran out of money. Momma would go down to the jetty and shout across, but he never answered and nobody else did either. She was just some mad woman shouting across the river and people gave us a wide berth. The house fell into disrepair because it always was on the edge of falling apart and poppa was the only thing keeping it together. When he stopped doing that, everything began to fall apart.

"Marti? You OK?" Sammy snapped his fingers rapidly in front of me. I blinked. "Earth to Marti!"

I looked over and shot him some sad side-eye. "Yeah. I'm good. It's just… it's a lot, y'know?"

"Sure. We'll be there soon. Won't take us long to say our last goodbyes." He immediately back-pedalled when he saw my scowl forming. "Of course, though, take as long as you want. We can wait."

I sighed and pointed down at my leg. When Sammy shot me back a quizzical glance, I rolled my trouser up just over the ankle, where my spanking new experimental ankle bracelet was flashing double-green. "Can't stay too long. I don't know what happens if I don't get back to the prison tomorrow but I can't say I want to find out. Don't expect it'll be pretty." I'm not sure what he replied, but it came across as a non-committal "uh-huh." We didn't talk about my incarceration much, mainly because until now our communication had been limited to occasional phone calls or the prison visitor room. In particular, we didn't talk about what I'd done to get there. We never talked about that. The last time he visited must have been years ago. Forgive me, but it's been a long day so I can't remember when it was exactly but I'm assuming it must have been pretty much around the time that momma first got diagnosed, so that places it around the millennium. A new era, a new hope. Looking back now, it's insane that that's what people thought about some arbitrary turn of a calendar page, a man-made invention that does the simple job of marking our days and trying to instil them with some relevance. Not that we don't try that every new year, turn over a new leaf and all that, but this one was super-special, see, because it has more noughts at the end than usual and we haven't seen that before.

These moments we shared, those glances of unspoken sorrow, were suddenly lost when the raft jolted uncontrollably. My eyes darted around frantically in the half light, struggling to make out what obstacle we'd run afoul of. I couldn't see anything. Then, just as abruptly, it shuddered again. This time it came from directly underneath but up at an angle. The coffin started sliding away towards one edge. Sammy and I both reached over to it, but

178

that tipped the raft a little too far and one corner dipped fully beneath the water.

"That's Bessie." Joshua cursed loudly, "Get back! Or we'll all be in the drink. Keep it steady and keep quiet!"

None of those things were easy to do, but - startled out of our sibling stupor by the sudden movements - we just about managed. Momma stopped moving and so did we. Everyone breathed a sigh of relief, the only thing that could be heard over the buzz of insects and the gentle rocking of the raft.

"We're not too far now. Reckon we can make it without annoying her again." Joshua started pushing the raft out again with the long pole and insisted we be the ones to keep an eye on the water. "Not too far..." he said again, in a voice that offered reassurance but came out far too shaky and scared to manage it.

Sammy looked out over one side, I took the other, and Joshua stared straight ahead. I could make out the first few graves now, the tops of bamboo crosses barely visible above the yellow flecks of foam that had gathered around them that Sammy had told us earlier was toxic sludge. It gleamed unhealthily, lit by the low moonlight and the dim lantern held up by a thin pole on the corner of the raft. Nothing moved. Nobody said anything. It was one of those moments when everyone so expects something to happen - we were still high from the burst of adrenaline a few instants earlier - that we started to imagine things. Sammy reckoned he spotted a snake curling around a nearby tree, but that turned out to be a scarf. Joshua looked steady, but he was shivering underneath that cool exterior, shaking like a leaf after our lucky escape. I was squinting out into the swamp and jumping at every shadow. It might only have been a couple of minutes later when we ran into the first levee, but it felt like hours.

***

"Here. Tie that rope just there..." Joshua pointed at a tall, thin shape on the edge of a mud bank that rose from the surrounding murk. I could just about make out that it was some kind of hitching post and that galled me for a moment, because it meant that people had to have been doing this graveyard trip often enough for someone to have put it there deliberately and even though that was thoughtful of someone, it was clearly a reaction to whatever thoughtless decisions had led to the ever-flooding delta and the mangroves hereabouts being in such a mess. I threw the rope but missed. As we drew closer, I just leant in instead and reached up, putting the little loop over the top of the post like I was a kid at the state fair when the barker lets you cheat so you can win a giant toy. That's when I first saw it, just out of the corner of my eye, rising up from beyond a tree stump which, for all I knew, probably doubled as someone's grave marker. It was another human being, which surprised me since the raft was pretty much the only way to get out here. It shifted slightly on its feet, arms sticking out at odd angles like there were giant strings over its head held by a big hand directing its movement, y'know, like one of them puppets at an old-time

180

kid's show. I've never seen anyone move so janky unless it was poppa late one night after one of his benders. I called out, as much to warn the others as to greet whoever it was shambling through the fog, knee-deep in grey-green water. It turned its head toward us and then shuffled forward slowly, each step accompanied by a thick slurping of ooze from the muck beneath our feet, flecked through with foamy bubbles of that same yellow sludge we'd seen earlier.

It spoke. Or what was, perhaps, intended as a voice, used to be a voice, but now was only a low grunt like something you'd expect from a black bear jumping out at a startled day-tripper. I nearly withdrew in shock, only just remembering that two steps behind me there was a polluted river containing a hungry alligator.

"What was that?" Sammy looked over at the shape now approaching us, then back at me. Before I got a chance to reply, Joshua spoke.

"Ain't nobody supposed to be here. No way someone could have swum it, and I ain't taken anyone here in over a week, not since we brought Remi up."

Whoever - or whatever it was - drew a little closer. I could just make out an odd glint from its right leg, something silvery shining in the dim glow of the raft lantern.

"Remi? Hey, Remi, whatcha doing?" Sammy called out. It should have been a call that echoed eerily, something to match the surroundings in its spookiness, but it came out garbled, muffled, barely a croak.

"That's Remi alright. I'd recognise that artificial leg anywhere." Joshua had finished tying up the raft and stood now on what counted for dry land at the base of the levee, basically only half an inch of thick goop. "Something's wrong though. Something's very wrong." In contrast to Sammy's, Joshua's voice sounded low and panicked. He didn't need to say something was wrong, we could all hear it in the tone and pitch of his voice, in the clinging mist around us and in the water sploshing around the raft. Sammy, though, still voiced out loud the question on both our lips.

"What's wrong, Joshua? Wasn't Remi the last person you brought over here?"

"Oh, yeah, but that's what's wrong. We brought him here to bury him. Remi's dead as a doornail."

***

Whatever the thing was - and it sure looked like Remi - kept coming, ambling toward us. Occasionally the artificial leg would sink into the ground, and it would halt temporarily, unable or unwilling to think about how to extract itself from the mire. This gave us plenty of time to decide what to do, which turned out to be 'defend ourselves'. The long raft oar and the shovel on the coffin proved to be the only two things at hand which even remotely resembled a weapon. Sammi and Joshua grabbed those, which left me with wits and fisticuffs as my defences. Given that choice, I opted for fisticuffs, though I hoped I wouldn't need them. Whatever it was, I didn't want to get close enough to punch it and sure as hell didn't want those filthy nails and scum-stained mouth anywhere near open

182

skin. The body was close now, its groan a challenge to arms, its breath so foetid you could smell it even over the rank odour of the swamp. I looked around for any other weapon but every branch I grasped fell to pieces as soon as I touched it, dead wood in a dead place.

Remi lurched forward, his arms no longer flailing but very definitely reaching for a stranglehold, which caught Sammy off-guard and sent him pitching onto his backside in the mud. Joshua swung the oar round in a long, low arc and I could hear the crack where it struck the bone of his good leg. Attempting to capitalise on this success, he tried it again but the crack this time came from the oar. A good swipe, but Joshua had aimed it at the artificial leg which proved too much for the wood of the oar, which splintered near in half, the top third dangling by a few slivers of wood and the bottom half presenting as what could now serve as a reasonably effective spear. Still, it gave Sammy time to scramble back to his feet and assail Remi with a shovel to the face. He staggered back, but in anger rather than pain. I don't think the dead can feel pain. At least, I didn't then. I used that opportunity to vault past, behind Remi and up towards firmer ground, in the hope that I'd find something more useful to wield in the fight. What I found instead was that Remi wasn't alone. There were three, no four, more figures emerging from sodden graves, each rimed in stinking yellow foam and clearly but slowly shuffling toward us. I cursed out loud and turned around to shout a warning, just in time to see Remi fall beneath a rake of mud-caked fingernails, unable to utter even a solitary scream as he fell headfirst into the murky water. Sammy had followed up with a series of well-aimed blows, but they did little to slow Remi's assault. Cursing again, I rushed back, taking Remi by surprise as I grabbed the oar-spear and rammed it upward into his throat. It stuck there in his neck as he raised both his arms in a last-ditch attempt to remove it. There was no blood, just a slow trickle of tainted yellow liquid oozing from the wound. Sammi withdrew from the fight, panting and leaning heavily on his shovel, as Remi pitched forward, face down on top of the dead ferryman Joshua. There was a moment of respite, of silence before the coming storm, before more moans brought us back to the heat of the moment.

The oar-spear was useless now, but it had done its job. As Sammy tried to find solid ground to defend us on, I took the liberty to avail myself of a different weapon which had now just become available. I hurried to meet Sammy on a little mound nearby and we stood there, back-to-back, ready to repel whatever this profane place threw at us. Four figures approached which clearly had once been townsfolk, people we might have recognised from our youth, people we once laughed with, bought groceries from, spent time fishing with. Their features were erased now, rotting in their foetid frames, but I think I recognised Old Man Devereaux in his customary flat cap and breeches and Lavinia with her great hoop earrings and armfuls of fake gold jewellery. As dead and decrepit as the forms were, it was hard not to see their wretched forms as the people they had once been, people who had died and for whom Rest In Peace had proven to be nothing but a bad joke. Nevertheless, we sent them reeling with blow after blow. I'll say one thing for the elderly dead, they don't move any faster than they did in life, and I offered a silent prayer to that effect. Once we were done and the four of them lay dead, again, in the water at our feet, Sammy noticed for the first time what I'd been using as a makeshift club. His eyes widened.

"Seriously?"

"I didn't see you complaining when I was defending you against Lavinia's charms a moment ago. Besides, he doesn't need it anymore."

"I don't know what's become of you. Using a guy's artificial leg like that. It's enough to…"

"Can we quit soul-searching? We've got enough trouble here without having a conscience on top. It's kill or be killed at the moment, at least until we can get away or help comes. When it comes to that, I know which I'd rather choose." That's as close we'd come in all these years to discussing the murder that had sent me to prison.

***

"So, we're stuck here?"

"Looks like it." I'd tried to repair the oar, get the raft going again, but it was useless. What's more, none of the dead wood of the mangroves was long or strong enough for the task.

Sammy looked at me and I returned his gaze. He sighed, then turned away.

"What now?"

185

"We're still not going to talk about it, huh?" He spat on the ground, though whether it was out of disgust or just to get the taste of toxic sludge out of his mouth I didn't know.

"What is there to say?" I was hedging around the subject, I knew. I always had. There were things I didn't want him to know.

"I think we need to talk about it, Marti. We've never talked about it."

"And you think now is the best time?" I was indignant, but also exhausted, depressed and covered in mud. I didn't want to talk about anything.

"There's nothing else to do. Unless you've come up with another plan in the last few minutes."

I was going through Joshua's satchel, hoping to find something we could use. My hands closed around a bottle of whisky. I held it up in triumph. If Sammy was disgusted before, that was nothing to how he looked now.

"You wanna get drunk? That's never the answer. Figured you'd know better. It didn't help poppa and it won't help us. But sure, go ahead, drink your life away. I won't stop you." His shoulders slumped in defeat.

"A sip won't hurt. Besides, we've still got work to do." I motioned down to the coffin. "You promised momma. I may not agree that's the best place for her, especially not now, but a promise is a promise. And, as you've pointed out, we've got nothing better to do."

Sammy shrugged again, but this time moved in closer, stepping onto the raft. It shuddered slightly and something slithered in the water nearby. It was almost a comfort to be reminded that merely an hour ago all we had to worry about were snakes and a big ol' alligator. We grabbed one end of the coffin each and, with considerable grunting, managed to get it off the raft and make slow progress up the levee. We paused next to a dead, downed tree to consult the map, since we couldn't do that with our hands full of coffin, and agreed a way forward through the quagmire to a stone tomb we could see in the distant gloom which looked like it was close to the marker. We didn't see or hear anything else move around us as we sloshed forward, ankle to knee deep in foul swamp water, slowly up the hill to where poppa was buried.

***

There's no getting away from what happened next and no reason anymore to be coy about my crime. It'll be obvious to you soon, obvious in the way it probably has been to the smarty pants reader for quite some time.

I killed poppa. What's more, to protect Sammy and momma, I'd do it again. It was late one night and we should by all rights have been in bed except that momma was too tired to tell us what to do, so we just hung around, getting under her feet and under her skin, hoping that he'd come home in a good mood with presents for us or not come home at all. Well, neither of those things happened. He rocked up just gone midnight, eyes red and bleary, barely able to walk, soaking wet from the waist down on account of how the ferry hadn't been working so instead he'd waded barefoot across the bayou, drunk as a skunk. He'd been lucky not to fall arse over tit into the swamp, but somehow here he was, and he didn't look like he was feeling lucky. He railed at momma for not telling him the ferry wasn't working, as if that was somehow her fault, then grabbed another bottle and held it loosely in his right hand, taking large swigs in between shouts. Then he leaned in close and grabbed her by the neck, screaming in her face. I ain't never seen poppa that angry, I ain't never seen momma that scared, and I never wanted to again. Something changed in me, I reckon I was overtired and scared and stupid and a whole bunch of other things rolled up into one big ball of fury. I grabbed the bottle from his hand and brought it down on his head as he stood there, dumbfounded, covered in glass, his face a patchwork of red slashes. He dropped mamma and turned on me, but never got the chance on account of how I was much smaller, much faster and not pissed as a newt. As he pitched forward, I drew back and he fell forward, cracking his head open on the corner of the table. We all drew a quick breath in those few moments, a relief that the nightmare was over for the evening, before we realised that he wasn't moving and that he never would again, that the nightmare was over for good. It was only later, when the police came by and we tried to give our accounts, that it was clear a new nightmare was about to begin, for me at least.

I'm saying all this now, finally, because we were about to face that nightmare again. We should have seen it coming, really, what with all the other zombies we'd had to deal with, but here he was, wretched and stinking, standing tall before us. At least we knew for sure where he'd been buried now. I never did want momma to be buried next to him and if I'd gotten my way she wouldn't have been, and we wouldn't have had to face this. But, hey, nobody listens to me, I'm not the good kid anymore, just the neighbourhood murderer, the family black sheep, the one person nobody wants to talk about. Sammy looked up at him in fear, I looked up in anger. We didn't dare look at each other. That would have meant acknowledging the unfinished business between us.

It seemed certain he was going to move to attack, so we laid the coffin down as reverently as we could. We could clean the mud off later, before we put it in what clean earth we could find. Sammy still had the shovel strapped to his back and was trying to remove it quick-time, but with fear-struck fingers he was moving too slow. All I had was Joshua's satchel and Remi's leg, so I swung the former around my head with my left hand, moving forward slowly, trying to attract his attention to buy Sammy time. I didn't know how these things worked, what foulness in that sludge had awakened them from eternal slumber, but I thought I saw a brief flash of recognition in its eyes as it advanced on me, growling and groaning, splashing and sloshing through the moonlit marsh. I stood my ground, swirling the satchel, hoping to catch him with a blow to the head before I was able to clock him with the artificial leg. There was a strange noise and a flash coming from the water at my feet but I daren't let it distract me from this fight. I'd been wanting this fight all the time I'd been locked up. To face him again, adult to adult, to take him down properly, rather than to catch a lucky break as he fell but get blamed for his death anyway. It was the murder I was about to commit that I'd served my time for, not the one I'd committed as a kid, scared shitless and pounding my balled fists on my poppa's wounded head as he bled out on the floor. I relished it. I only wish he could have seen it in my eyes before my first blow sent him reeling into the water, staggering to keep upright. Sammy stepped forward then, spade in hand, grim-faced and quaking.

"Bro?" He didn't answer. He didn't need to. "I got this." As poppa bared down on me again, I swung up with the leg and heard a loud crack as his lower jaw broke off. It didn't even slow him down. Then he was on me, both of us wrestling in the water now, sending great splashes to each side. There was a red glow under the water, I wasn't sure where it was coming from and I didn't have much time to consider it. Only one of us had to come up for breath and that was me. If poppa could keep me under, keep that stranglehold up, I was a goner. I could hear frantic, muffled shouts from Sammy and feel where he was punching the water with the spade, hoping to land a deadly blow, but I could also feel the last breath leaving me. I couldn't let him win, so I tried to summon up the last of my strength and just managed to get my head above the water. To say I was surprised at what I saw would be an understatement.

Some few paces behind Sammy, up on the little rise where we'd left it, momma's coffin had slid down into the scummy, stagnant water and was slowly sinking. Then, with a loud popping noise, the lid burst open and out came momma, white-shrouded in the silvery moonlight, thin as a rake and ready for vengeance. Like I said before, I don't know what rules these things played by but if I had to guess, I'd say it had to do with how long they'd been dead. I'm sure I saw a brief flash of recognition in those eyes before she launched herself into the fray, bypassing Sammy and sinking her teeth into poppa's leg as he pulled me back underwater. I'm sure that's what saved my life. The pair of them went down into the muck, arms locked around each other's throats. I stood shakily and coughed up blood, water and whatever yellow gunk was swirling around in the muck. Sammy just stood there crying.

We never saw either of them again. Whatever he'd done to her in life, I like to think she repaid in death. That would have been justice. As much as we'd wanted to bury momma, there was no trace of her body once the thrashing in the marsh was over and the water once again took on that calm, yellowish sheen. Whatever currents there must have still been had washed them both right away.

That should have been the end of it. That would be a fitting end - a just end, even. If anyone made a movie of this, that's where it would finish, in that moment of calm at the end of a long day. Roll credits, close curtain. Except, life isn't that simple. Sammy pointed down in the water and I could see that flash of red again. It was coming from my ankle bracelet. No matter how quiet or still we tried to be, no matter how slowly we moved, it was like a beacon to anything that was underwater and that included a great big alligator, which we could see now, sliding down off a bank before it was completely submerged. Our evening wasn't done.

***

We'd had enough trouble trying to fend off long-dead townsfolk and our own poppa. We'd exhausted ourselves wading through the swamp with a heavy coffin on our shoulders. But it seemed fate had one more surprise in store. There was only one course of action available to us when we saw the alligator start swimming over to us: we fled. If we could get to higher ground - hell, if there was higher ground anywhere to get to, we could maybe fend it off at a distance before those snapping jaws closed on our legs. It was a miracle we managed it. Really, we should thank Joshua. Firstly, because the zombie that used to be the ferryman chose that moment to close in and attack us but got between us and Old Bessie. So, when her jaws first gripped a leg and crunched down, that wasn't on either of us. It took her a while to get the recently dead flesh clean from her mouth and by then we'd managed to haul ourselves on top of the stone tomb nearby that we'd been heading to earlier with the coffin. Bessie swam around in the muck below, evidently upset that she couldn't quite reach us. The second thing we had to thank Joshua for was that bottle of whisky. We didn't sit there and drink it, tempting as that would have been. Instead, when Bessie began slapping the stony sides of the crumbling tomb with her massive tail, I broke the bottle over her head while Sammy used what was left of the lantern to set fire to it. I'm sure she survived once the initial shock of her head being on fire had worn off. She'd probably be fine again as soon as she was back underwater, but it did make a good sight to see her thrashing around in the mud whilst she tried to get back into the river. We both sat there on the tomb, drenched in sweat and swamp water, hoping nothing else would come, but wondering how we'd manage to get back home.

That's when I remembered my ankle. It was flashing quicker now, two bright red dots, a warning not to me but to whoever was monitoring it. Permitted range exceeded. Permitted duration exceeded. Prisoner escaped. Use all available means to locate and retrieve.

***

So, we sat there all night, just the two of us, bloodied but not broken. We laughed and cried and chatted and hugged like we'd never see each other again. Just how brothers are supposed to behave. Then, just as the sun rose over the delta in all its morning glory, we heard the low thrum of an approaching chopper and soon after the searchlight fell on us, spent and exhausted, lying on top of the old Devereaux tomb like we'd just passed the night in the cemetery for fun like we were kids on a dare and I didn't even care that they'd sent a chopper after me because though it was taking me back to the joint, for now it meant freedom and that's all I hoped for in that moment.

In the end, it's not about the zombies. It's the grim horror of knowing just what ordinary people are capable of doing to one another and that is far, far, worse. That's the whimper the world ends with, the thousands and thousands of little cuts we inflict uncaringly on each other day after day and then forget about. Each knife that cuts a little deeper, each blade that twists a little more. Our bodies are full of those unseen wounds. We had just endured a particularly deep cut, blood spilled by blood, but what brought us to that was everything we've done as a species to get to the point where folks have to swim across a river of toxic sludge just to get to their dear departed Excuse my language, but that's just fucked up. I ended up paying the price for the lives I wrecked. I can't imagine that the people that wrecked the lives of everyone else in our town will ever pay such a price, but maybe that's just me.

***

THREE DAYS LATER

She's never been this far upriver before. But there's something there. Something calling to her.

From her vantage point on the riverbank, she can see it. A huge wall of stone, impenetrable and glistening with the morning dew. At the base of that great wall, which spans the entire width of the river, there emerges a steady trickle of water which feeds the delta she once called home. Beyond it, she cannot see, cannot imagine.

Thankfully, she doesn't need to. Several men dressed head to toe in orange move around the river at the base of the dam, occasionally prodding the river with long poles and taking small samples of the yellow muck that sticks to its base. Perhaps they

194

don't know what they've done. Perhaps they don't care.

She doesn't care either. All that she knows is that she's hungry. It's a different kind of hunger than she's used to. Everything feels different now. Her face is covered in a mass of burn and scar tissue. She swims slower than she used to. None of that makes any difference, because all she has is hunger.

Old Bessie, dead but still walking, waddles back to the edge of the river and slips slowly, silently, into the water and makes her way upriver to where the men gather, unaware of what fate awaits them.

Meet The Authors

Carl Hughes

Carl is a writer and journalist who has worked for the national and provincial press in the UK and has had his articles published worldwide, from the UK to Australia, India to the US. His fiction has appeared in many anthologies and magazines and he has won numerous writing competitions. He specialises in writing about the offbeat and bizarre, with a special love of horror and Twilight Zone-type stories. He is married and lives in Norfolk with wife Linda.

Chris Rodriguez

Chris Rodriguez has retired from the horrors of conventional life. She now lives on the brink of inspiration in a 100-year-old cottage in Pocatello, Idaho. Her works have appeared in print and online in various formats and themed anthologies including Rhetoric Askew, several by Horrified Press/Thirteen O'Clock, Left Hand Publisher's, Mindscapes Unimagined, ParABnormal Magazine, DL Russell's Nobody Goes Out Anymore, Gravestone Press, The Writer's Prison's Second-Hand Creeps and Blunder Woman Productions, Wrong Turn, which has recently won Best Audiobook Anthology at the SOVAS Awards.

John Kujawski

John Kujawski has interests that range from Guitars to The Incredible Hulk. He was born and raised in St Louis, Missouri and still lives there to this day.

Liam A. Spinage

Liam A. Spinage is a former philosophy student, former archaeology educator and former police clerk who spends most of his spare time on the beach gazing up at the sky and across the sea while his imagination runs riot.

Olivia Arieti

Olivia Arieti lives in Torre del Lago Puccini, Italy, with her family. She writes drama, poetry and fiction. Her stories have appeared in several magazines and anthologies including, Enchanted Conversations, Enchanted Tales Literary Magazine, Fantasia Divinity Magazine, Forgotten Tomb Press, Horrified Press, Infective Ink, Pandemonium Press, Sirens Call Publications, Blood Song Books, Black Hare Press, Pussy Magic Magazine, Stormy Island Publishing, Breaking Rules Publishing, Scarlet Leaf Review, Iron Faerie Publishing, Dark Dossier Magazine, The Chamber Magazine, Paramour Ink Press, Raven and Drake Publishing.

Paul Edwards

Paul Edwards is a life-long horror fan, and writes his own twisted tales in any spare time he can grab. He has seen three collections of stories published—Now That I've Lost You (Screaming Dreams), Black Mirrors (Rainfall Books) and Night Voices (Demain Publishing), the latter being a joint-collection with author Frank Duffy. Paul is a big fan of rock music, role-playing games and rough Somerset cider.

Rickey River Jr.
Rickey Rivers Jr. was born and raised in Alabama. He is a Best of the Net nominated writer and cancer survivor. His work has appeared in the JJ Outre Review, Stellium Literary Magazine and Fabula Argentea (among other publications).

Rie Sheridan Rose
Rie Sheridan Rose multitasks. A lot. Her short stories appear in numerous anthologies, including Killing It Softly Vol. 1 & 2, Hides the Dark Tower, Dark Divinations, and On Fire. She has authored twelve novels, six poetry chapbooks, and lyrics for dozens of songs. She is also editor-in-chief for Mocha Memoirs Press and previously served as editor for the Thirteen O'Clock imprint of Horrified Press. She is on X and BlueSky as @RieSheridanRose.

Stephen Lang
Stephen Lang has harboured a lifetime love of all things terrifying. His short stories have appeared in the BHF Book of Horror Stories (BHF Books), Step Into the Light (Bag of Bones Press), Dark Stories Volumes 3 and 4 (Gravestone Press), Fear

Forge (Horrorsmith Publishing), Halloweenthology: Dia de Muertos (Wicked Shadow Press) and online at The Sirens Call and Unveiling Nightmares. Stephen lives in Bristol and is a member of the Horror Writers Association.

Susan E. Rogers

Susan E. Rogers lives in sunny St. Pete Beach, Florida, USA transplanted from Massachusetts. Her move was the catalyst to focus on her life-long ambition to write. Her other interests include genealogy and psychic spirituality, often twisting these into her writing. She self-published her first book in 2018 about her own psychic experiences, published an occult thriller with an indie press in Sept. 2023, and an occult mystery is under contract for release in 2024. Starting in 2020, her short fiction has been published in print anthologies and several literary and genre magazines, including Cobra Milk Literary, Bluing the Blade, Luna Station Quarterly, and Horror Tree's Trembling with Fear. website: www.susanerogers.com